Two Old Men and A Fish
A Fisherman's Tale

Wayne E. Lofton

© 2017 Wayne E. Lofton
All rights reserved.

ISBN: 1977978703
ISBN-13: 9781977978707

Other Titles by this Author

Jamie And The Little People
My life with Jamie and his family of little people

Jamie, The Little People and Their UNDER-GROUND WORLD
Volume two

Jamie and the Little People and the Passage of Time
Volume three

Corky's and Wally's Fishing Adventure
Children's Book

I would like to dedicate this book to Ray Hammer, who was the first and original owner of the Nestucca Valley Sporting Goods Store in Hebo, Oregon.

He was an excellent fisherman and a good friend who left a hole in many lives, including my own, with his passing.

Ray Hammer

TO MY READERS, YOUNG AND OLD

Being an avid outdoorsman and fisherman almost my entire life and having been in the company of many others in the same category after serving in two states as a trooper assigned to Fish and Game Enforcement and spending twenty-five years as a fishing guide in the state of Oregon, I can honestly say that a number of events have happened to me or in my presence involving very large fish that, when hooked, left the area without being seen, to the dismay of the angler.

One such incident occurred in November 1976 while I was fishing for salmon on the Tillamook River in Oregon.

The river was high and muddy, almost in flood stage. I had been fishing with a large bait of salmon roe, letting it lie on the bottom, when I hooked a very large salmon.

I fought it for ten minutes without being able to see it, suspecting that maybe it wasn't hooked in the mouth because I had absolutely no control of the fish.

There was an old man fishing in the same place. I knew his name because he lived close by, but I've forgotten it now. He had helped me land a large Chinook salmon the day before in the same part of the river. Anyway, I asked him if he would look down into the water from the high bank that we were on as I backed up. I wanted him to try to see where the fish was hooked when I lifted up hard on the pole.

He was doing just that when he looked back at me and said, "Son"—I was a lot younger then—"ease off the pole. That's a huge salmon, and it's hooked in the mouth. It's a lot bigger that the one you caught here yesterday."

He no more than said that when the fish turned and left downriver. I had no way of stopping him, and he took all the line on my reel with him.

By the way, the large salmon that I had caught the previous day with the old man's help weighed fifty-eight pounds.

I hope you enjoy the story. Good luck fishing.

The River

CHAPTER 1

The old man was getting tired. He had been fighting the fish for probably two hours, but he wasn't sure. He was glad the fish had decided to lie still on the bottom for a while. The old man needed a little rest. He had already had a cramp in his right arm, which had been extremely painful. But he hadn't given up, and it eventually went away. He had been a little light headed too, but that had also diminished since he'd quit running up and down the riverbank chasing after the fish.

He had decided to go fishing that morning at the spur of a moment. He hadn't planned it; in fact, he had even left his landing net at home, so "if and when" he got the fish close to shore, he was going to have to try to beach it, which was going to be a difficult task because he could hardly bend over as it was.

It was a beautiful day in late September—no wind, blue sky with a few floating clouds. That was the main reason he had decided to go fishing. When he got out of bed this morning and saw what kind of day it was, he kissed his wife, who was still in bed, good-bye. Then he grabbed his fishing pole, and out the door he went.

Of course, he did stop by his shop and grabbed a container of cured salmon eggs and a container of live sand shrimp from the refrigerator. Eggs and shrimp were about the only bait the old man ever used for salmon since he had been a young boy. It worked well for him, and he wasn't going to change. Of course, there were many, many other things to use: spinners, herring, and various kinds of wobblers, just to name a few, and he had used them all at one time or another. But his favorite was shrimp and eggs.

When fishing for salmon in the fall, he usually always used his larger pole and a bigger reel. He also used heavy line. It was an eighty-pound test braided nylon that he customarily used for bobber fishing because it floated and didn't drag in the flow of the water, like monofilament did. Also, monofilament had to be waxed frequently to make it float, which was a real pain. He also was using about three feet of thirty-pound test Maxima monofilament leader. In other words, he was using "pretty strong" equipment. He shouldn't have any trouble landing the fish as long as it stayed in the immediate area and stayed out of any logs or big rocks on the bottom of the river.

The old man had arrived at the fishing hole just about one hour after daylight, after paying two dollars in the can and walking about a quarter of a mile across the farmer's private property. He had fished in this place hundreds of times but usually from a boat; rarely from the bank. He knew in his own mind that probably at least five boats had already fished the hole before he got there. They would have been in a hurry, trying to race one another downstream, trying to be the first to a fishing hole. He knew because he used to do the same thing.

He also knew that the water was clear, and any fish that had arrived the previous night after coming in from the ocean and traveling the approximately five miles upstream to get there would be skittish and, upon seeing the boats traveling over them in the river, would be reluctant to bite. He figured that after the boats left and the sun was full up, they would settle down and lie on the bottom in the deep water or stay hidden under the fast-white water in the riffle.

When he first got there, he stood for a long time and just looked at the river and listened. It was his favorite time of day. The birds were singing everywhere, and there was a multitude of insects flying around—bees, mosquitoes, and dragon flies, just to mention a few. A couple of mallard ducks had floated downriver and were swimming around on the far side, doing what ducks do.

After standing there for ten minutes or so, he turned around to fetch his pole and fish bag, which he had left up the bank from the water's edge. As he was walking away from the water, he heard something behind him. He turned around and caught movement in the riffle, low down, almost to the deep part of the hole. It was a large movement—not a fish jumping, but a push of water like what a seal does when it moves fast after a fish. He said out loud to himself, "Darn, I hope that isn't a seal."

If it was, there would be no fishing that day in that part of the river, and he knew that it wasn't unusual to see them that high in freshwater. He had seen a lot of them that far up in the past.

Years ago, when he was young, farmers and fishermen used to chase and shoot seals when they came that far upriver to feed on salmon and steelhead. But now they were protected by law and had been for many years, so they could do basically whatever they wanted. And they did. Down in tidewater, about two miles up from the ocean, the old man had lost fish to seals while they were on the line. In fact, more than once it had happened.

The old man reached down and picked up a large rock. He considered throwing it into the river to try to scare the seal back downstream, and then he would just go back home because if, in fact, if there was a seal there, the fish wouldn't bite. He just stood still, waiting for the seal to show himself. A seal is a mammal; it must come up for air, but it can hold its breath for a long time.

He waited, alert and quiet, for about five minutes and never saw any movement. He finally dropped the rock but still stood looking at the water. Finally, deciding it must have been a beaver or otter and that it had crawled out into the grass on the opposite shore, he turned back around and walked to his fishing pole and bag.

Of course, his pole was already rigged for fishing with a two-ounce bobber and weight, three feet of thirty-pound test leader, and a number 4/0 hook. He took his bait container out of his bag and put a sand shrimp and some cured salmon eggs on his hook. He made a half hitch from the line above his hook and tightened it around the bait to hold it on the hook. Then he walked back down to the water's edge.

The old man looked at the water. He knew where to cast; he knew where the fish would be lying. He had fished in this place numerous times.

His bait was the best he could use. He pumped his own sand shrimp from the bay and kept them alive in his refrigerator. He cured his own salmon eggs from the fish he caught. He also had made a liquid scent from the sand shrimp. He kept the scent in his refrigerator to keep it fresh. He put it on his bait just before he cast into the water. The scent was not only an added attractant, but it also masked the human and any other smell on the bait.

The old man was an expert in what he was doing. He knew what to use, where and when to use it. There were salmon fishermen as good as he was, but definitely no one any better. He had been doing this a very long time and his memory was excellent. He could almost remember every large salmon he had ever caught and where he caught it.

CHAPTER 2

The old man stood at the edge of the river again, this time with his pole in his hand. He adjusted his bobber stop so that his weight would drift approximately three feet under the surface. That would make his bait drift along the bottom in four feet of water, which was how deep the fast water in the riffle was.

He figured there might be a salmon in the riffle, but it was doubtful. The first boat that had come through would have scared the fish down into the deep part of the hole. The salmon would have been in the riffle during darkness, and at first light, they would have still been moving upriver after coming out of the ocean. In the past, they had even run into the old man's boat when he startled them before sunrise.

The main reason for casting in the shallow riffle was so he wouldn't scare any fish hanging at the upper end of the deep hole. He very rarely cast into the deep part of the hole first; it was just his habit not to do so.

The bobber, weight, and bait hit the water with a small audible splash in the quiet morning. The bobber then went upright, as it should, and started drifting downriver. It went about six feet and jerked sideways but didn't go underwater. The old man got ready to jerk, but the bobber continued without any further movement. Figuring it was a small trout or salmon smolt, which is a small juvenile salmon, he reeled his line in.

His eggs were almost pulled off the hook, and his sand shrimp was gone. A salmon smolt or trout had not done that. As he held his hook in his hand, he looked out across the river and smiled. He knew what had done it. It was a jack salmon, which is a small, two- to four-pound salmon that has spent only one year in the ocean and has come back early.

Now he knew for sure there was no seal in that area, or the jack salmon wouldn't have hit his bait.

The old man put on new bait and cast out in exactly the same spot. The bobber floated all the way to the slower deep water without any movement. He started to reel in, and three things happened almost at once. First, the bobber went down, clear out of sight. Second, he jerked so hard that he almost fell back on the ground, and third, he noticed three or four small fish, probably smolt, jump out of the water at the same time.

He had jerked too fast without reeling all the slack line in first; consequently, he hadn't hooked the fish.

With a bobber in fast-moving water, the weight and bait create a drag in the water, so the floating line to the bobber has a tendency to bow out. The line must be straight to the bobber to hook the fish when it is jerked.

This is very elementary, and all fishermen know it, but the excitement of seeing the bobber go clear out of sight unexpectedly sometimes overpowers common sense.

Trying to get control of the situation; untangling his line, which was wrapped all around him and his pole; and saying a few impolite words under his breath, he remembered the little fish jumping out of the water at the same time in a little bunch. This was unusual and indicated that a predator was after them.

He still hadn't seen a seal, and he hadn't seen any birds or otters that might be after the little fish, so it really meant only one thing: there was a big salmon in the deep water that moved fast enough to scare the little fish.

Most people don't know that a big salmon coming out of the ocean will strike a salmon smolt or trout, especially if the little fish looks wounded. The old man had seen this happen two or three times when a small fish was hooked and being reeled in to be released. Whether the salmon struck the little fish to eat it is unknown. Maybe it looked like a small fish the salmon had fed on in the ocean.

Anyway, the old man had seen small fish jump out of the water many times while fighting a big salmon, so he knew that they were definitely instinctively scared of them.

While putting another bait on his hook, he noticed his hands were shaking a little—not a common thing. He knew what was happening. He knew what was in the hole, and it made him nervous. It always did, every time.

There was a big Chinook salmon in the hole. He didn't know how big or how many, but it was nice to know they were there. Just because it was the right time of year and the river condition was good, it didn't mean there were fish in every hole. A fisherman likes to know that he is fishing for something.

If he had been in his boat, there would be no problem. He had a fish finder mounted in it. The one he owned now wasn't as accurate as the ones he had used before, but it worked sufficiently to tell if a salmon was under or beside the boat. He didn't have one for fishing off the bank.

The old man finished baiting up. Before he cast, he looked up onto the river and decided to change his strategy a little.

His bait had been floating about four feet under the surface, like he wanted. That was about right for the riffles, but the bottom dropped off sharply just before reaching the calmer and deeper part of the hole. Undoubtedly, at least some of the fish were lying in this spot and would be deeper than his bait was floating, so he moved his bobber stop farther up his main line. Now his bait would float about six feet under the surface.

He had to use caution in doing this because he did not want to get his bait traveling under the level that the fish were lying in. Salmon and steelhead will lie almost directly on the bottom in shallow water or the riffles, but in deep water, they lie at various levels. This is probably due to various reasons, such as water clarity, temperature, and depth. Also, if they are resting or on the move, feeding and the amount of daylight are major factors.

He knew he didn't have to put his bait right at their level, but close. Salmon and steelhead will not dive for a bait floating down a river—at least he had never seen or heard of it—but they will swim up.

He lifted up his pole and got ready to cast, but before he let go, there was a big disturbance in the water. Just about directly in the middle of the hole, there appeared a huge boil, or uplift. The old man saw a flash of silver under the surface at the same time but then thought he was just imagining it because it was immense, way too big for a salmon. He couldn't see as well as he used to anyway, and the sun was coming up, creating a glare on the water. He figured that was probably what it was.

This time he cast his bait and bobber at the bottom of the riffle, just as it entered the deep hole. The bait and weight went down, and the bobber stood upright. It drifted about three feet and went sideways. The old man jerked. There was no slack in the line this time, and the line went tight with a fish on.

CHAPTER 3

After only a few moments, the fish jumped out of the water, and he could see that it was just a medium-sized jack.

He let the fish wear itself out, and then he pulled it up onto the sand where he was standing. He had no intention of letting it go; jack salmon were excellent eating. He had eaten a lot of them over the years, and there was no doubt that this one, having just come in from the ocean, would really be good. His wife knew just how to cook them. She filleted them and put them in a big frying pan with a lot of young green onions out of their garden. She fried the fish slowly with lots of butter and seasoning. Sometimes she added sour cream just before serving, but not always. When salmon have been in freshwater awhile during the fall, when the river is usually rather colored or muddy, the fish will pick up a small amount of the muddy taste in their meat. If sour cream is added after the fish is cooked, it takes away this taste. Garlic will also mask this flavor.

Of course, nothing would probably be added to the fish the old man had just caught, since it had just come out of the ocean and was bright as a silver dollar.

He dispatched the fish swiftly and laid it in the grass next to his fishing bag.

He picked up his pole and started to rebait.

Hearing a noise, he looked upriver and saw a boat coming around the bend just above the start of the fast water, so he didn't cast. It was a fiberglass drift boat, white in color with three occupants, the operator in the back and two individuals up front. He knew the boat and the owner. His name was Al, and he didn't like him much.

The old man thought Al was a loudmouth braggart, and he had had words with him before on the river. Al thought he knew everything about fishing and life in general and wasn't shy in letting everyone know it. Some people just acted like they owned the river, and Al was one of them. He was a fishing guide who worked in the area most of the time.

Al was approximately forty years old and single. He had been married once, but his wife had left him. The old man could understand this. He figured Al had just talked her right out the door. He had met her one time when he ran into Al and her at the Hebo Sporting Goods store. The old man thought she was a good-looking, smart young lady and liked her immediately. He thought she was too smart to be with a guy like Al. Turned out that the old man was right. She finally wised up and left.

Actually, the old man thought Al was a pretty good fisherman and fishing guide no matter what he thought of him personally. His clients seemed to like him, and he caught quite a few fish.

The boat came over on the old man's side of the river, being courteous and staying out of the fishing hole.

When it got up beside the old man, Al said, "Good morning, old timer. How's the fishing?"

Of course, the old man immediately took offense. He knew he was old. Didn't really care, but he didn't like people like Al calling him old. They had a way of making it sound like an insult.

He said "morning," but he didn't smile.

Al added as they floated by, "I suppose you would get pissed if we anchored down at the deep end and fished the deep spot, huh?"

The old man said, still without smiling, "Suppose so. I would appreciate it if you just kept on movin'. There's lots of river ahead of you yet, and I can't go nowhere but here. Not walkin' too good these days."

Al looked past the old man and saw the jack salmon lying up on the grassy bank and said, "I see you got one. How many do you need?"

"More than one," he replied.

Then Al said, "Well, maybe we'll just anchor anyhow. What are going to do about it? Go home and get your boat?" And he started laughing.

The old man just looked at him a moment until Al stopped laughing, and then he said, "You know, I thought there was a seal out there a minute ago, and I picked up a big rock to throw at him. I think he seen me pick it up and left because I never seen him again. I still know where that big rock is, and I know you don't have much sense, but I'd hope you have as much smarts as that seal because a boat makes a lot bigger target than a seal does."

The two men up front in the boat, who had been grinning, stopped, and Al quit smiling.

The old man couldn't hear what the men said to Al, but he heard Al say, "Of course the old son of a bitch means it" and "Damn, he wouldn't be fishing here unless there was a bunch of salmon."

He could then hear Al saying to the men that he had told them to hurry up and get their gear in the boat so they could leave this morning—see what happens?

The old man stood there and watched the boat go down around the next bend in the river. Al was still talking away and waving his arms when he wasn't rowing.

The old man kinda smiled and said to himself, "Damn, I just don't like that guy."

CHAPTER 4

The old man got ready to cast again. He was glad Al had kept the boat out of the fishing hole. At least he hadn't scared the fish too bad, he hoped. The fish had seen the boat go by, for sure, but it didn't pass directly over them.

He wasn't in any hurry to cast yet, giving the fish a little time to settle down just in case.

Some very little fish, about two or three inches long, were trying to jump up and grab a bug across the river. The bug was about as big as they were, so they weren't being too successful at it. The old man was watching them and meanwhile watching the deep water for any movement. None came.

When he cast this time, the line jerked, jerked while he was casting, and the sand shrimp went flying across the water, off the hook. The line must have bound up on the reel spool when he was bringing in the jack salmon

He was starting to reel in when a huge boil appeared where the sand shrimp had fallen into the water. The old man said, "Good Lord." He couldn't see the fish, but the turbulence in the water said enough. He thought the fish would have to be enormous to cause that. In fact, he had never seen a salmon cause a boil like that in his life. A big sturgeon on the Columbia river, yes. But a salmon, no.

Whatever it was, it had caused mud and silt to come up to the surface from the bottom, and the water had to be at least fifteen feet deep in that spot.

As he rebaited, he thought about what it could be. A sturgeon, maybe, but he had never heard of one coming clear up into the river. He had heard of a few being caught down in the bay, but not in the freshwater of the Nestucca.

This time the cast went perfect, just where he wanted it, at the top of the deep hole but still in the current. The bobber went upright and started to float out into the slower water, and then it started to move sideways over to the far side. It didn't really bob up and down or have any jerky movement.

The old man knew exactly what it was. A fish had been lying just behind where he had cast. The bait had drifted directly in front of it, and it had taken the bait in its his mouth, slowly moving forward and then off to the side. The fish wasn't in a hurry. It had gotten what it wanted.

The old man knew it was a salmon. He had seen them take the bait like that many times. He jerked hard, setting the hook.

The fish went crazy, and water flew. The salmon may have taken the bait slowly, but it wasn't moving slowly now. The old man's reel was hissing. He reached down with his left hand and tightened up his star drag to increase tension. He wanted to wear the fish out, and he knew it wouldn't break the line—or at least didn't think it would. Anything could happen, though.

He had been fighting the fish for about five minutes and hadn't seen it yet. The salmon was running from one end of the deep water to the other and at one time went upstream in the fast water for thirty or forty feet before the old man got him turned around and headed back down.

He knew the fish was hooked legally, in the mouth. He could feel it throwing its head back and forth. He didn't think it was a real big one, but he hadn't seen it yet, so he wasn't sure. The fish stayed mostly in the deep water and down close to the bottom.

Chinook salmon are power fighters. In other words, they rarely fly out of the water, airborne like a steelhead or Coho salmon, unless they're snagged in the body somewhere. They'll do it, but they would rather use their powerful body and thrash around on the surface trying to dislodge the hook or stay down as deep as they can possibly get. And they are good at what they do. Salmon probably get things in their mouths all the time that don't taste good or don't feel good, and they must get rid of it.

The old man had seen this several times. The salmon seem to push water back out their mouth and shake their head at the same time, and they like to do it while they're thrashing around on the surface. It's a harrowing experience to be holding onto the pole while this is happening. If it's a big fish, a fisherman feels as if his arms are being pulled from his shoulders, especially if the salmon is close.

The old man had waded out into water about four feet from the gravel bank. He didn't want the fish to get into the shallow water yet—not until it was worn down a little, anyway. He had had that happen before, and it usually wasn't a pleasant experience.

He had heard of a man who got hurt very bad trying to land a big Chinook salmon on the Trask River one time, years ago. He got the fish in the shallows before it was tired, and the fish went crazy. The guy apparently got too excited, which is easy to do, and jumped on the fish, which is a definite no-no. He dropped his pole and tried to grab the line with his hands while also trying to get control of the fish by grabbing it through the gills. He jumped on and straddled the fish in an attempt to control it.

Well, the Chinook salmon, supposedly a forty-plus-pound fish, decided it didn't like it. Consequently, it turned around and went back downriver and in the process about drowned the man before he could get free. The man lost one finger and dislocated a shoulder in the process.

The point being, don't put your hands on a salmon unless it's tired and allows you to do so. The old man knew this, so he was not going to pull the fish into the shallow water by the bank until it was tired and ready.

Another five minutes of dogging around in the deep hole, and the salmon came to the surface. The old man could see it quite well. It was not thrashing as expected or lying over on its side but just holding upright and barely moving.

The fish was definitely a Chinook salmon. The old man could easily tell that, and it was probably in the neighborhood of twenty-five to thirty pounds. A good-sized fish, but no monster. It was in perfect condition, having just arrived from the ocean.

The old man thought it was probably rather tired from fighting its way upstream all night and that was the reason it wasn't fighting harder. He decided to start trying to pull it closer to bank, and he put on more pressure.

The fish, shaking its head a little, allowed itself to be pulled around and led toward the old man and the shore.

◆

CHAPTER 5

The old man started to back up, wading backward out of the water, pulling the fish toward him and the shore as he went.

He then reeled fast and walked toward the fish and back out into the water as he did so.

This time when he stopped, he was about five feet from the fish, and he could see his hook in its mouth. The old man got a shiver on the back of his neck. The hook was in the lower left jaw but not in the jaw itself. It was in a loose piece of skin. A very small piece of skin that had been ripped from the inside of the jaw.

The old man still had quite a bit of pressure on the pole and had just started to back up again when the fish went crazy. It stood right up on its tail in the shallow water and started shaking its head.

A whole bunch of things happened all at once. The hook, of course, came loose. And since the old man had so much pressure on the pole, it, accompanied by the bobber and two-ounce weight, came straight at the old man. It was too close to duck, even if he did see it coming. It just happened too fast.

The bobber hit him in the face, just to the right of his nose, making a slapping sound when it made contact. It was light in weight and didn't do much damage except sting a little.

The two-ounce weight, on the other hand, hit him directly in the middle of his chest. It made a loud thud when it hit and hurt like the dickens. It made him sit right down in the water, at the edge of the bank, fast. He didn't lose consciousness, but it sure made him light headed and dizzy. He lay back on the bank and then started feeling around for the hook. He didn't remember it hitting him anywhere. That's where the real danger is in incidents like this, and he knew it. He had had hooks embedded in his fingers and hands and one time in his ear.

A big salmon hook, usually a 4/0 or 5/0, does not come out of the flesh easily, and it hurts—really hurts. Also, a tetanus shot is required, which the old man didn't particularly care for either.

Anyway, he found it with the bobber and weight lying in his lap and off to his right side, not stuck in any clothes, or, thank God, flesh.

He sat up and decided to get out of the cold water. He wasn't very wet—just his seat—but when he stood up, some of it ran down into his hip boots, which wasn't a pleasant feeling.

He picked up his fishing pole, which was lying half in and half out of the water, where he had thrown it when he fell backward.

Standing there and looking out over the river, he felt quite miserable. His chest still hurt. In fact, his whole body hurt. He contemplated going home.

He wished he hadn't lost the salmon, but things like that happen. And it really wasn't his fault; he knew that. It just wasn't meant to be.

Walking up on the bank with his back to the river, he heard a big gurgle or rush of water. Turning around, he spotted another huge boil at the bottom end of the deep spot.

He couldn't believe what he was looking at. He knew the salmon he had just lost could not make a disturbance in the water like that. That fish was only twenty-five or so pounds and maybe thirty-six inches long at the most. No way. It just couldn't do it. Whatever had caused that uplift of water had to be huge.

He kinda got the shivers and knew it was not just from being a little wet.

He said out loud, "Aw, heck with it," and started to reach for his bait container. But then he thought he had better check his leader first. It might have been frayed from the salmon's teeth, which it was. He walked over to his fishing bag, got out his spool of monofilament leader, and made up a new one. And then, as he was baiting up, he said to himself, "I'm not going home just yet."

Before he cast again, he looked out over the water, as usual, and thought, That fish wouldn't be lying where that boil was. It must be lying midway in the deep part of the hole. It probably got startled by the splashing in the water made by the fish that came off the hook and turned swimming downriver and then turned again, fast, at the end of the hole, making the big whirling boil.

So the old man moved his bobber stop farther up his line so the bait would be about eight feet under the surface. And then he cast to the head of the slower water, just above the deep part.

CHAPTER 6

The bobber went upright and then went flat on the water and then upright again. It did this a couple of times before it stayed upright. The old man knew what it was. The bait and weight were dragging on the bottom where it was shallow at the upper end of the hole. He had planned it that way, so the bait would float out to where the fish was instead of dropping down from the surface. He was trying not to scare the fish.

He drifted his bait through the hole five times. Nothing touched it. The bobber never dipped, moved sideways, or anything. He wasn't disappointed; he wasn't sure the big fish was a salmon anyway. He knew there wasn't a seal in the hole, or the other salmon that he had hooked wouldn't have bitten.

If it was a sturgeon, he doubted that he could get it to take a bait on a bobber. Sturgeon are bottom feeders. They have a mouth like a big tube for sucking food off the bottom.

He thought seriously about taking his bobber off and letting his bait sit on the bottom. Years ago, that was how he fished for salmon—never with a bobber—and sometimes he still did that, especially from his boat.

It was a totally different way to fish than he was doing now, but if there was a sturgeon in the hole, he probably would take the sand shrimp, since that was one of the main sources of food for them in the bay.

He reeled in and stood there looking out over the river. He thought, "Darn. I'm getting too old for this. I'm tired!" He really considered going home.

He decided to try it one more time, so he took off what was left of his old bait and started to put on new. And then, looking up at the river again, he decided not to put on salmon eggs, just a big sand shrimp.

He cast in the same spot as before. The bobber went upright and started to float through the deep part of the hole, and then it just stopped. It didn't bob or move to the side; it just stopped and started to drag down a little, as if it was hung up on the bottom. The old man knew it couldn't be the bottom or a snag. He had floated through the same spot too many times for that to happen.

He braced himself and then jerked just as hard as he could possibly jerk, almost coming off the ground.

It came up so solid that he lost his balance and fell over a little. He caught himself and looked up at his pole. It was bent almost double, with the line extremely tight.

There was no movement. It was like he was hung onto a log or something else secured to the bottom of the river.

He held it like that for some time, and when there was still no movement, he started giving it a little slack line and then little jerks, trying to figure out what was going on, thinking maybe he was hung up on something.

He continued for approximately three or four minutes and then, after not feeling any movement, decided to try to break his line. He let his pole go out straight and then, after tightening his star drag, started backing up the riverbank attempting to break it or pull it loose from the bottom.

That was when it happened. He was down on his knees, getting pulled straight into the river before he could get his drag loosened up. The fish shook his head, and it felt as if the old man's arms were coming out of his shoulders.

He finally got stable and in control of himself and said out loud, "Oh, my God," as the fish tore around the deep hole, making the boiling disturbance at the bottom end that the old man had seen earlier.

Mud was clouding the water all over the deep part of the hole. As the old man held on to his pole and tried to keep up with the fish, he noticed there wasn't just one boil in one place but many boils everywhere. Old dead and rotten leaves were mixed in with the mud and brought up to the surface.

He still hadn't even had a glimpse of the fish that was staying near the bottom. He knew one thing: whatever it was, it was huge.

It might have been exciting, but still he was a little bit apprehensive. He figured that he would probably never land the fish, especially by himself. But he would sure like to see it before it came off the hook or his line broke.

CHAPTER 7

The old man's name was Johnathon Pane. He was seventy-two years old and lived in Hebo, Oregon, with Lucy, his wife of thirty-two years. Hebo was just a bump on the map with a grocery store and a sporting goods store. Just the kind of a backwoods place where an outdoorsman would live. The only notable thing about Hebo was that it sat at the crossroads of State Highways 101 and 22, which made it convenient for the residents of the area to travel west another ten miles to the Oregon coast or east twenty miles to the Willamette Valley. Also, Tillamook was a short drive north on Highway 101 and Lincoln City to the south.

Another thing about Hebo was that it lay within the Nestucca Valley a short distance from the Nestucca River; consequently, the major business was the sporting goods store, where the old man had worked as a fishing guide for twenty-five years prior to his retirement two years ago.

Before he became a fishing guide, Johnathon had spent time in the army and had worked for various mills and timber companies around the Tillamook area.

He had worked for one logging company, felling timber until he had an accident and broke his leg in three different places. That had put an end to his logging career. He had walked with a limp ever since.

Johnathon and Lucy had three children—two boys and one girl; and two grandchildren, both girls. They were extremely proud of all of them.

They all lived in the Willamette Valley, on the other side of the coastal mountains. Consequently, Lucy was usually in the valley visiting the kids and grandkids, leaving Johnathon to his life of fishing.

Lucy didn't like to fish much. She liked to cook and eat them but preferred to leave the catching to Johnathon.

She even liked the climate better in the valley since her arthritis had started acting up a few years ago. She would like to move over and be closer to the kids and live in less rain but knew she could never get Johnathon away from the Nestucca River.

They weren't hurting for money because neither one of them was a big spender or had expensive tastes. They had never bought a brand-new car or pickup, instead settling for a good used one when need be.

They were receiving monthly checks from Johnathon's disability and retirement plan and Lucy's retirement from being a teacher for thirty years, so money didn't seem a problem.

Neither one of them was a big traveler anyway. They preferred family, longtime friends, and the state of Oregon to far-off places.

Johnathon, except for a recent hernia operation, a shoulder operation, and high blood pressure, was still in relatively good shape for a man that age. At least he had thought so up until about a half hour ago.

The old man had been an avid fisherman since the age of seven and had caught his first fish in the Nestucca in that year with his dad. It was a trout. At the age of fourteen, he caught his first steelhead and one year later a salmon, both in the Nestucca.

The Nestucca River was not the only river the old man had fished. He had fished and guided on most of the rivers in Northwest Oregon, but he always had lived within traveling distance of the Nestucca River while he lived in Oregon, which was most of his life.

He had caught many fish, salmon and steelhead mostly, no doubt numbering into the thousands. The second year that he was a fishing guide in Oregon, he caught and/or landed over five hundred pounds of Chinook salmon during the fall season for himself and his clients. He had recorded the numbers and poundage every day in a book and was surprised at the end of the season with the total. It made him change his guiding strategy. From that year on, he gave his clients a full-day fishing trip, sometimes catching their limit and sometimes not, but never again just going out to kill fish as quickly as they could and sending them on their way.

In later years the big thing was to catch and release the fish so fishermen could fish all day and catch as many as they wanted. When the salmon and steelhead are on their spawning run from the ocean and are thick in the rivers, this can be accomplished, especially with a good guide who fishes every day and knows where the fish are and what to use to catch them.

Someone invented this idea, probably a wildlife biologist or fish-and-game employee, with the theory that if the fishermen kept fewer fish, that meant fewer fish to be raised in the hatcheries and more to reach the spawning grounds. Consequently, more money saved by the department.

There was a major problem with this as far as the old man could see. Not all released fish live to reach the spawning grounds. In fact, a good number die shortly after being released, the main reason being hemorrhage. Anytime a salmon or steelhead is hooked in the gill structure and fights hard, it starts bleeding—he had never seen it stop after being released—and the fish dies. More fish are hooked this way with bait than with lures, but he had seen it also happen with lures.

One time the old man was fishing on the Nestucca with two clients in the drift boat when he noticed a large salmon floating belly up, coming downriver toward his boat. He netted the fish and tried to revive it, with no success. Approximately ten minutes later, he could see another floating down, out of his reach, about twenty feet away. About a half hour later, a boat came by from upriver with two occupants. The boat operator, who knew the old man, was a guide, and he told them they had caught four fish just up and out of sight around the bend and had released them. Both men were drinking beer and appearing to be having a good time until the old man told them about the two salmon that had floated by dead. He made the men row over, and he put the fish that he had netted in their boat and asked if they recognized it. They said they did, and the old man told them to record the fish on their card, as required by law, and to learn how to release a salmon unharmed if they didn't wish to keep it. Chastised, they did as the old man said and left downriver. Just before they were out of sight, they waved back at the old man with their middle fingers up.

The old man had suspicions that a lot of salmon, even if they weren't hooked in the gill structure and bleeding, didn't make it to the spawning grounds.

A fall salmon doesn't eat or consume any nutrients on its spawning run up the rivers, and he knew they didn't because of all the salmon he had cleaned, he had never found anything in their stomachs. They must take bait and lures into their mouths out of habit, anger, or some other reason no one is aware of. Anyway, it would take some doing to swim up a river where they were born and to spawn, let alone be hooked by a fisherman and fight to near death and be released.

CHAPTER 8

Johnathon had two boats that he guided with. One was a twenty-one-foot Smoker Craft sled with a 125-horsepower Mercury motor, a jet pump, and a nine-horsepower trolling motor. The second one was a twenty-foot Koffler drift boat with a Minn Kota electric motor.

Both boats had dual electric anchor systems and could hold four passengers besides him.

He had owned many boats over the years, but these last two, which he used primarily for guiding, were his favorites. He had a fish finder in each boat, and they worked quite well. They both had side finder capabilities, which meant they could spot fish from either side of the boat out to the riverbank. Some people didn't believe in them, but Johnathon swore by his.

To prove a point, one time about eight years ago, Johnathon was anchored in what was known as the flats. It was about a one-half-mile stretch of the Nestucca

River that ran flat, with no turbulence and no deep holes. It was probably one hundred feet across and no more than six feet deep anywhere in that one-half mile.

It might have been reasonably shallow, but the salmon loved to lie and rest there on their way upriver, especially if the water was a little high and colored. The guides knew this, and so did a lot of other fishermen who fished in the area.

Johnathon was anchored about one-third of the way through the flats with two customers aboard.

A friend of his, who was also a guide with two customers that day, was anchored about twenty feet to his side.

Everyone had a pole out and was having a good time chatting and so forth.

Now, Johnathon's fish finder covered the water to either side of his boat and under it, but not to the front or the back.

Johnathon heard his fish finder beep, which indicated a fish was in the scope. He looked over at the screen, saw that the fish was passing on the left side of his friend's boat, and told him so.

His friend, whose name was Jim, reeled in his pole fast and lowered his line down into the water where Johnathon indicated. In a manner of seconds, he had the fish on and handed the pole to one of his clients.

This happened again not more than ten minutes after they landed the first fish. The same circumstances.

Johnathon told Jim, in jest, he wasn't going to tell him again. He could find his own fish. Everyone had a good laugh over that.

Johnathon had sold his jet sled and big drift boat after retiring. Now he owned a small sixteen-foot sled with a twenty-five-horsepower Honda motor. It worked just fine down in tidewater and for trout fishing in the lakes, but, of course, it couldn't be used up in the river system. That was just fine with Johnathon. He kind of enjoyed fishing from the bank, like he used to do when he was a kid. The boat traffic on the rivers was getting horrendous anyway.

The last year he guided, it seemed like he was having words with some other boat operator about once a day. Nothing usually very serious, just stupid things that got Jonathon's dander up, like throwing empty beer cans out of their boat or dropping their anchor on top of Johnathon's clients' fishing lines, which was a definite no-no.

Of course, as he got older, he lost his patience more easily. So, things that didn't bother him ten years ago seemed to irk him now.

CHAPTER 9

The old man still had the fish on his line. It had made some strong runs around the hole, and then it would lie still for a period of time and occasionally shake its head. Johnathon was tired. He felt pain in many places on his body where he never had before, one of which was his chest, which rather bothered him.

When a person gets older and gets any pain around his chest, his first thought is of his heart. And Johnathon was no different, although he figured it was probably from the sinker that had hit him earlier.

He really didn't know how much longer he could continue. Fighting a fish like the one he had on would have been difficult twenty years ago, let alone at his age now. He decided to slack off a little on the pole and line. The strong tension he was using didn't seem to bother the fish anyway. It was just wearing him down.

He thought maybe he should cut his line and let the fish go. But that was something he had never done before, and he didn't particularly like the idea, and besides, the line left in the fish could tangle up with something and possibly kill the fish. Doubtful, but anything could happen.

What he really wanted was to see the fish or whatever he had a hold of. Of course, he knew it was a fish, but he wasn't sure what kind of fish. He just couldn't believe it was a salmon. He should have seen it by now, and it was too big, in his mind, to be a salmon.

He was standing there, in water halfway up to his knees, wondering what he was going to do. If the fish wouldn't move, how was he ever going to tire it out, so he could control it or even see it?

He heard a noise upstream around the bend. Another boat must be coming. That was all he needed—somebody trying to tell him what to do and getting in the way.

He backed up on the bank, hoping that when the boat came down, it would come close to him. He would lift his pole so the boat would go under and on downstream. That way it wouldn't be out in the deep part of the hole and scare the fish. All he needed was for the fish to get really spooked and head back to the ocean. There was no way he could stop it, and he might just lose his pole in the process. That would really make a bad day out of a not-very-good day.

Johnathon could see the boat coming out of the corner of his eye. It had no passengers; just the operator.

As it got closer, Johnathon was still looking out into the hole, at his line, and a voice said, "Hey, old man, do you think that snag is going to go away, or do you want to get in the boat and go out and try to get loose from it?" And then the man laughed real loud.

Johnathon recognized the voice and quickly turned toward the boat and said, "Oh, God, Cork, am I glad to see you. Pull that boat up on the beach and come over here and help me. I'm about all done in, and I got a cramp in my left arm."

It was Wayne Lofton. His nickname was Corky, given to him when he was an infant. It had nothing to do with fishing, and now he wasn't laughing anymore. With a worried look on his face, he beached his boat, jumped out, and ran for Johnathon.

Cork Lofton was a good friend of Johnathon's. In fact, probably his best friend. They had known each other for at least forty years. Cork was seventy-two years old, the same age as Johnathon.

Cork, unlike Johnathon, had done many things in his life. He had spent four years in the Coast Guard, worked for the states of Oregon and Alaska as a state trooper, and, like Johnathon, had been an Oregon fishing guide for twenty-five years before he retired.

He first met Johnathon when he was a young man working for the fish and game division of the Oregon State Police, living in Tillamook.

Johnathon at that time was working for one of the lumber mills in Tillamook. He was single and fished every spare minute that he wasn't working at the mill, and that was what he was doing when he and Cork first met.

He was fishing at the Rock Hole of the Trask River, having gone there when he first got off from his job.

Since the Trask River ran through Tillamook Valley close to the mill where he worked and he had only about two hours until dark, it just figured that was where he would be.

He was fishing for salmon, of course, and had just laid his plunking rod down on a rock and picked up his drifting rod. He was thinking about a girl he had met just a couple of days prior and forgot to reel in his plunking rod before he cast the other.

OK, now, in Oregon, you are only allowed to use one pole and one line when fishing for salmon, and after Johnathon cast, he realized what he had done. He laid his drifting pole down on the same rock, picked up his plunking rod, and commenced to reel it in.

He saw a movement out of the corner of his eye and, turning, saw Cork, who was in the full blue uniform of the Oregon State Police, standing about twenty feet behind him, and he was not smiling.

Johnathon, knowing what it looked like and knowing that he could get a ticket for using two poles and maybe even get his fishing license suspended, which would be an utter disaster, got all shook up and dropped the pole that he was reeling. The reel hit the rock that he was standing on with a loud bang, and the reel handle busted off and went flying into the river.

Johnathon, totally flustered, just stood there, turning red and looking down at his pole, not saying a word.

Cork asked him for his fishing license. Johnathon, while getting it out of his wallet, said, "I really wasn't fishing with two poles."

Before he could explain any further, Cork said, "I know. I've been standing here watching you fish for a couple of minutes."

Seeing Cork's name tag on his uniform, Johnathon said, "Thanks, Trooper Lofton. I really appreciate it."

Cork, holding up his hand, said, "No problem, but you might reel in your plunking rod before picking up your other rod next time." And he smiled great big.

That encounter started a friendship that had lasted for years, and many a time they would rehash the first time they met.

Cork would always tease Johnathon by saying he should have given him a ticket and had his license suspended for a year, that it sure would have saved a lot more salmon to get up the rivers to spawn. Johnathon would chuckle and say, "You ass."

CHAPTER 10

Now Cork, having been a first responder most of his working life and having taught first aid classes for the Red Cross in his spare time when he was a fishing guide, didn't like the way Johnathon looked when he got to him.

Johnathon pushed the pole at Cork, and he took it, keeping pressure on the pole and line but not knowing why. He was worried more about Johnathon than anything else.

Johnathon, grimacing, immediately started rubbing his arm and knelt down to rest. He never said a word.

Cork asked Johnathon if he wanted him to break the line or try to get it loose.

Johnathon looked up and said, "Hell no. There's a fish on the end of it. Just keep the line tight. I'll be rested in a minute and take the pole back."

Cork looked down and said, "If there's a fish on the end of this line, it must be wrapped around a snag or a big boulder, John. Hell, it's not moving at all."

Cork was turned sideways to the river, standing at the edge, and he had just finished saying that when the fish shook its head so violently that he tried to hold on to the pole. In doing so, he tripped, lost his balance, and fell into the water on his fanny. Meanwhile, he was screaming "Jesus Christ" and then, "John, what the hell have you hooked into?"

Cork, in trying to get upright and out of the water, all the while trying to keep the line tight to the fish, somehow lost his cap and got his head soaked. He stood there, holding the pole and muttering unintelligently, with water dripping off his nose and chin.

Meanwhile, Johnathon, who was sitting down now, not kneeling, was breaking up with laughter and saying he had never seen footwork like that in his life.

That got Cork laughing too, and he had to admit that it probably looked a little bit foolish; that was for sure.

He looked down at Johnathon and asked him, "Did you see the fish? It almost had to be a salmon, and it must be hooked right in the front of his upper or lower jaw for him to be able shake his head like that."

Cork said, "I've never felt that strong a head shake in my life, from any kind of fish, sturgeon or any other."

The fish had quit shaking his head and was lying still again while Cork kept strong tension on the line.

It was quiet now, with neither man saying a word nor moving.

Finally, Cork asked Johnathon what he was doing down at the river anyway. Cork had asked him to go fishing with him the day before, but he'd said he couldn't.

Johnathon said that when he had gotten up this morning, Lucy and he hadn't seemed to hit it off just right, so he thought he had better put some space between them. And besides, the weather looked good, and he felt like coming to the river.

He was still sitting down, and he looked up at Cork, who was looking at him and grinning.

Cork, who knew Lucy well, said that he could totally understand.

Cork had known Lucy just about as long as he had known Johnathon. In fact, he had been at their wedding. He also knew they loved each other immensely and always had but had to have their own space as well.

Now, Cork's wife, Linda, was a little bit different. Very rarely did he go fishing or hunting anywhere without Linda, and if truth be known, she outfished him on most fishing trips, which created a lot of humor between them. When they went in the boat, Cork was always rowing, and he would put her in the best position to fish the hole. They both knew he did that but never brought it up.

Of course, she usually hooked the fish, which was fine with Cork because he ran the boat while she fought the fish. And then, when it was time, he netted it.

They worked in perfect harmony, and it worked just great, with very rarely a mishap.

But as close as he was with Linda, he also knew that sometimes she needed a little space. And that was when he would go fishing with Johnathon or Wayne Jr., and Linda would go shopping, visit a friend, or just stay home and sleep in, which she loved to do.

CHAPTER 11

Cork first met Linda in Alaska after he left Oregon with his fourteen-year-old son and joined the Alaska State Troopers.

He lived and worked out of Juneau at first, but after three years, he was transferred to the fish-and-game enforcement office in Sitka.

It was a Friday in February when he received a complaint at a small Indian village named Angoon, which was on Chatham Straits, midway between Sitka and Juneau.

Since there was no mail flight from Sitka to Angoon that day and the state trooper pilot was off duty, he was either going to have to wait for Monday or go by water, which was a good hour or more.

There were a several of boats available for use at his office, but Cork was the only trooper in the office, so he decided to go by himself in an open eighteen-foot

Boston whaler, which is a seaworthy small boat that one person can handle easily.

Cork arrived in Angoon around noon and completed his business in about two hours. He left immediately for Sitka, but since it was February, darkness caught him about three miles out of Sitka, and the temperature had dropped well below freezing.

Now, Cork was used to traveling in an open boat during the winter months, and he had all his cold-weather gear on, including a foul-weather suit, face mask, and heavy gloves. But it wasn't stopping hyperthermia from setting in.

This had happened before, but usually in daylight hours. He would pull the boat up on some beach and start a small fire to warm up. But he didn't do it this time.

He figured that he was only about fifteen minutes or so from the office, and he could make it before it got pitch dark.

He made it, all right, but he was in full-blown hyperthermia when he got to the state trooper dock, and he had trouble tying the bow line to the cleat on the dock. His mind was fuzzy, and he could just barely walk.

He got to the office door, which had glass in it, and he could see the coffee pot on. But he just couldn't get the key in the door lock. His fingers wouldn't work.

He decided to break the glass with his elbow to unlock the door. He knew it would set all kinds of alarms off, but on his last attempt with the key, it worked.

He got a cup of coffee, burning his mouth because it was too hot, and tried to drink and get his clothes off at the same time. He almost fell a couple of times before he got in the emergency shower, which was there just for that reason.

When he first got in the shower, it felt scalding hot, but actually, it was on cold. He stayed in the shower for fifteen minutes or so, and when he started shaking, he got out, put his robe on, and sat down at his desk with his coffee.

He drank two cups of coffee, which tasted terrible because it was bitter and black from being left on all day. Cork wasn't much of a coffee drinker anyway and never had been, but he knew he had to get something hot into his stomach.

When his shaking started to subside, he called Linda for messages. She was the answering service for the trooper office when it was vacant.

Cork had been at the Sitka office for two years. He had talked to Linda on the phone probably three or four times a week but had never had the opportunity to meet her. He knew she was a single parent, having lost her husband in a boating accident a few years before, and he knew she ran a chain-saw shop and answering service by herself. But he had no idea what she looked like.

When Linda told him there were no messages, he told her about his trip to Angoon.

In fact, he told her everything, even getting hyperthermia.

There was a big pause on the line, and finally Linda said, "That was really a stupid thing to do, wasn't it?"

Now, Cork wasn't used to anyone talking to him like that, and all he could say was "Really?"

She said, "Yes, really!"

Linda usually had Cork's working schedule, so she knew where he was most of the time. She said, "Don't you teach a class at the trooper academy, something to do with hyperthermia and cold weather survival?"

OK, Cork almost hung up. But he meekly said, "Yes." And that started a conversation that lasted fifteen or twenty minutes and ended with them deciding to meet at a local nightclub in Sitka that evening because neither of them was supposed to work the next day.

Cork, not liking blind dates and having had a couple of drinks too many and being in a state of anxiety, was standing up and talking to some friends when Linda walked up behind him, touched him on the shoulder, and asked, "Are you Wayne?"

He turned around, looked Linda in the face, knew immediately who she was because of the description she had given him, and fell in love. Apparently, she did too, because they had been together ever since. And that had happened thirty-some years prior.

CHAPTER 12

Linda met Lucy, Johnathon's wife, when she and Cork first came down from Alaska, and they immediately hit it off. They were both high-spirited women married to avid outdoorsmen, so they had a lot in common. Over the years they had become quite close and were always in contact.

Cork knew that if he told Linda about Johnathon's condition when he got home, she was going to tell Lucy, and poor Johnathon was going to catch it when he arrived home.

When Cork looked down at Johnathon again, he decided to keep the pole awhile because Johnathon still didn't look good. He looked pale and flushed at the same time and was still rubbing his arm.

Johnathon tried to stand up, and Cork told him to sit still and get his energy back, that he looked exhausted. Johnathon admitted that he was, saying he hadn't fought a fish that long in years, and he went on to say that at first, he thought it was snagged but after the head shakes decided it wasn't.

Cork grinned and said that it was hooked in the mouth—there was no doubt about that. He added that it seemed strange that it hadn't tried to leave the hole or shake the hook by thrashing out of the water.

Johnathon agreed and added that it must be one hell of a big fish and that the hook must not be hurting it at all, or, he thought, it would be more active.

Cork started to pull back hard on the pole with all his might while Johnathon watched, but the fish didn't move at all or even shake his head. Finally, Cork slacked off and said "Good grief" while rolling his eyes.

He said that if they didn't get that fish moving, it would never tire out, which Johnathon already knew, of course. Cork was just thinking out loud as usual.

Cork asked Johnathon if he had ever felt the line rub on the teeth when the fish shook his head, because he hadn't, and Johnathon said, "No, not at any time."

Cork, thinking out loud again, said that the line must be in the upper or lower jaw where it wasn't crossing any teeth, which would be a good thing. He didn't think the leader would last that long before breaking if it wasn't.

He asked Johnathon if he had thirty-pound test leader on, as usual, and Johnathon assured Cork that he did. Then he gave Cork a funny questioning look and asked, "Do you think I'm an idiot?"

Cork, looking down, said, "Of course not. I just wanted to make sure. And don't be so testy."

Johnathon apologized, saying he just didn't feel very good. Cork told him that he understood.

Johnathon stood up, and Cork, with the pole still in his hand, looked out into the river and said, "I think the fish is moving a little upstream."

They both were looking out in the river where the line entered the water and agreed that it had moved about two feet.

Cork had just handed the pole back to Johnathon and told him that he was going to pull the boat farther out of the water in case they had to get around it when Johnathon said, "Here he goes."

The fish started swimming steadily upstream, not very fast but not hesitating either.

Both men, not saying a word, started moving too.

They had just walked around the bow of Cork's boat when he told Johnathon that he didn't think the fish could get upstream because the water was so shallow that he had scraped bottom with his boat coming down over the upper riffle that was just below the bend.

There were two riffles above them in sight. Since it hadn't rained for some time, they were both shallow. The first one had about two feet of water, but the upper one was only about six inches deep.

Cork, who had been a game officer a good portion of his life and had walked these rivers at night looking for set nets and fish poachers, had seen lots of fish move over riffles this shallow with no problem. In fact, several times he had been wading across the really shallow ones and had startled some fish who, in turn, had almost knocked him off his feet.

But that had always been at night. The only times he had seen them move over the shallow areas during the daylight hours were either in the tidal area or when the river was rising rapidly after a heavy rainstorm. Neither was the case now.

The fish got to the bottom of the first area of shallow water and hesitated for a couple of seconds, and then the river erupted. Water flew everywhere. The fish traveled up about twenty feet into the shallow water and then turned and sped downstream.

Neither Cork nor Johnathon got a good look at it, but they both saw that it was a salmon or a fish that looked like a salmon, and it was huge. It was so large that it was almost impossible to believe that it really was a salmon.

Johnathon, who had had the pole in his hands during the fish's run upstream, had nearly fallen down several times because the rocks were so slippery along the river's edge. He had been running with Cork at his side, trying to keep up with the fish and trying to keep pressure on the line with the pole. A couple of times, Cork had grabbed Johnathon by the arm to keep him upright.

When the fish turned to head back downstream, he went fast. The shallow water must have scared him, because he didn't waste any time getting back to the deeper water.

As Johnathon and Cork tried to keep up, they noticed the water was in a turmoil. Small waves were lapping up on the bank, and mud and dead leaves were coming up from the bottom everywhere because of the turbulence.

The fish reached the deeper water but didn't stop. It continued to circle and thrash. It was either scared or extremely mad.

It must have known it couldn't go back downstream because it was shallow down there too, just not as fast. It had come up from there the previous night and remembered.

Standing on the bank again, by Cork's drift boat, Johnathon and Cork stood there quietly, trying to catch their breath.

Finally, Cork said while still panting, "I'm getting too old for this crap, and you are too." He looked over at Johnathon, who looked back at him, and they both started laughing.

Johnathon, still laughing, said that he had never even heard of anything like that, let alone seen it and been involved in it. Cork agreed that he hadn't either.

In all the moving about the fish was doing, it still would not come up to the surface so the men could see it. They had gotten a glimpse when the fish was thrashing to get up through the shallows, but that was all. They couldn't even really tell if it was a salmon. All they could see was it was a great big shiny fish. Of course, it didn't help that the sun was in their eyes shining off the water.

Now the fish started to slow down a little. Not from being tired—it didn't show any signs of that. It just seemed to calm itself.

It continued to shake its head now and then, not so much from pain but knowing it had something in its mouth that was an irritation or didn't taste good. So it was trying to get rid of it.

Cork, still standing by Johnathon, asked, "Do you really think you're going to land that thing? You're never going to get control of it. It's way too big for that. Hell, John, I don't think we could even get it in a net. And if we do get our hands on it over here near the bank, it'll probably hurt us both."

Johnathon turned his head toward Cork and said without smiling, "Cork, I'm going to land that damned fish whether it kills me or not."

Cork muttered, "Well, it just might do that, Johnathon."

The fish stopped swimming and held still in the same place it had earlier. It was the deepest part of the hole, so it was the logical thing to do.

Cork asked Johnathon if he wanted him to take the pole again. Johnathon turned as Cork continued, saying that he was going to have to leave because he had promised Linda he would be home to take her to their grandson's football game, and he was already going to be late as it was.

Johnathon handed the pole to Cork and started rubbing his arm again, saying, "Sure wish you didn't have to go. Might need that boat before this is over. If that fish decides to go downstream, I think I'm going to be in big trouble."

Cork shook his head in agreement, telling him that if that happened, there would be no way to stop him even with a boat, that the fish could swim a lot faster than he could row that boat, even downstream. Besides, "I need the boat to get back down river to my truck, so I can get home."

Cork said that he didn't think the fish would turn back down because it had had its chance when it was tearing the river apart a while ago, and it never even attempted to go down below the deep hole. It probably remembered how shallow it was down there.

Johnathon, having finished stretching and rubbing his arm, took the pole back from Cork and asked him if, when he got home, he would call Lucy and tell her what he was doing.

Cork turned to him and asked, "Why don't you call her on your cell phone?"

Johnathon said, "I fell on it earlier, before you got here, and I broke it."

Cork stood there for a second, looking at him, and then, shaking his head, said, "Good God." He reached into his coat pocket, got out his cell phone, and started to hand it to Johnathon.

Johnathon, holding the pole with his left hand and waving off the cell phone with his right, said, "No, no. You call her later, when you get off the river. If I call her, she's going to be mad at me and tell me to cut my line. And I'm not going to do that, damn it. I'm staying with the fish."

Cork put his cell phone back in his pocket, muttering "Good grief." And then he said, "OK, I'm out of here. I'll be back as soon as I can." And with that, he started pushing his boat back out into the river.

As Cork and the boat were floating downstream, he looked back and said, "John, don't do anything stupid, now. If that fish decides to leave, let it go."

Johnathon never answered. He just smiled and looked back at the river where the fish was and thought, The hell I will.

CHAPTER 13

Cork got downriver as fast as he safely could and took his boat out at the Cloverdale boat ramp, where his pickup and trailer were parked. Before he had launched his boat that morning, he had arranged for his vehicle and trailer to be shuttled from the Farmer Creek boat launch parking lot to the Cloverdale boat launch parking lot by the people who worked for the Hebo Sporting Goods store.

He lived in Dallas, Oregon, which was about an hour's drive over the Coastal Mountains from Hebo.

Cork and Linda had moved all over and lived in several communities since coming down from Alaska. Both were good with their hands in carpentry and building, so they would buy a home, recondition it, sell it for a profit, and move on to another. Meanwhile, Cork worked at being a fishing guide, and Linda worked full-time in retail. Consequently, they had lived in eight different communities since moving back from Alaska and had made many friends.

Their last move had brought them to a small farm outside Dallas, and that was where they decided to stay until they were too old to take care of it anymore.

Anyway, as Cork was leaving Cloverdale, he decided not to call Linda and tell her what was going on and have her call Lucy.

He had to drive right by Johnathon and Lucy's house on the way home but didn't think it was a good idea to stop and tell her what Johnathon was up to. If he did, she would drive down there and make Johnathon cut his line or something, and that would not be a good thing. Besides, if he didn't tell Linda where Johnathon was fishing, she couldn't tell Lucy.

His plans were to get home, unload his boat and gear, tell Linda the whole story, and get back to Johnathon as soon as possible, which was still going to take up to three hours. Wow, that was a long time, but there was no other way to do it, as far as he could see. Linda was still going to be upset with him because he had promised to be home in time to go to the football game, but not nearly as mad as she would be if he just called her on the phone.

It took nearly an hour for Cork to get home, as expected, and he was hurrying to put the boat and fishing gear away in the shed when Linda came out of the house.

Walking up to Cork and giving him a hug and kiss, she asked him how his day had gone and if he had caught anything.

Cork immediately started apologizing for being late and told her the story about Johnathon and the big fish on the Nestucca River. He was blubbering like an idiot when Linda held up her hand for him to stop, which he did, and he just looked at her.

She said, "if you had called me, I would have told you that the game had been canceled, and you could have stayed there with Johnathon."

Cork stopped what he was doing and stared at her for a second and then muttered, "Oh, shit." He hurriedly unhooked the boat.

He ran for the bait refrigerator, grabbed a can of Mountain Dew, and ran for his pickup, which was still running with the door open. He yelled back at Linda and asked her if she would finish cleaning up the boat and gear and clean the two salmon that were in the fish box in the boat.

Linda was smiling until he said that.

Cork didn't look back. He jumped into the pickup to take off and then hit his brakes, rolled down the window, and yelled at Linda, "Honey, I forgot. Would you call Lucy and tell her the story and tell her not to worry. I'll be with Johnathon."

He knew Linda had yelled something, but he couldn't hear what she said.

CHAPTER 14

This reminded Cork of an incident a few years back while he was still guiding.

It was late October, and he was going to meet a party on the lower Nestucca River and take them salmon fishing.

He had launched his twenty-foot sled and was tied up to the dock, waiting for his clients to show up. It was still dark and raining hard, with a slight wind of about ten miles an hour.

The wind and rain were hitting him in the face as he proceeded to put his two electric boat anchors over the side of the boat and run them up with the winches. He had no light, and the wind must have thrown a loop of the quarter-inch anchor line around his left index finger, because when he heaved the twenty-pound anchor over the side of the boat, it took his finger off at the first joint. He never saw it again; presumably, it went into the river.

There was very little pain. He canceled his guide trip, went to the emergency room in Lincoln City, came back, loaded his boat back on the trailer, and drove home.

The doctor said he couldn't use his left hand for about a month. He bandaged his hand up, gave him a tetanus shot, and told him not to get it wet.

Cork got home and told Linda what the doctor said. It was the last week of deer season, so they decided to go deer hunting.

Linda took a weeks' vacation from the store she worked in, and they went to the coast. Cork and Linda owned some property in the Hebo area and they had a travel trailer parked there, so they decided to stay in the trailer for a couple of days and hunt on their own property.

The first night in the trailer, it stormed the entire night, and it was still blowing and raining the next morning.

Cork decided to walk into the mountains anyway, so he got a big plastic freezer bag and taped it over his injured hand and left just as it was light enough to see.

Linda said that there was no way she was going out in that storm. She decided that the warm, snuggly bed was just the place for her to be, so she told Cork to take one of the walkie-talkies, and then she rolled over and went back to sleep.

Cork had gotten about one hundred yards from the trailer when he came face to face with a large buck. It was storming so hard he had trouble seeing the buck, and it was only about thirty feet away. The rain was hitting him in the face as he put the rifle up to his shoulder.

He had trouble seeing the deer at first because his scope was partially fogged up, and he couldn't grasp the forestock with his injured hand because it was taped into a plastic bag.

Cork finally got the cross hairs on the deer and pulled the trigger. Well, since Cork didn't have a good grip on the rifle and his rain gear was slippery on his shoulder, the rifle, in the process of discharging, flew back. The scope hit Cork between the eyes, and he momentarily lost sight of the deer, blinded.

Now, Cork had woken up with a sinus headache that morning, which definitely did not help matters.

There he stood, in the rain and wind with a blinding headache, his rifle hanging from his right hand with the scope full of water by now, and he was soaked to the bone because there was no way his rain gear could keep all the water out, and Linda was calling him on the radio wondering what was going on because the shot had woken her up.

He told her what had happened, and she begrudgingly said she would get her clothes on and come and help him look for the deer, just in case he had accidently hit it.

Cork looked for the deer for approximately ten minutes before Linda arrived, and they never found a trace of it. Linda asked where the deer was when he shot at it, and he showed her what had happened, including the lump between his eyes.

Linda went over to where the deer had been standing, walked around for a few minutes, and then yelled at Cork, who had been looking in the opposite direction. "Here it is."

Cork walked over to her. The deer was lying in a small ravine, partially hidden by a lot of tall grass. It was only about twenty feet from where he had shot it. He told her that he had walked by that area at least five times and had never seen it. Of course, it wasn't as light then, and the storm was worse.

They pulled the deer up onto flat land, and Cork took his knife out and opened it. He looked at the deer and then at his bagged-up left hand and then at Linda, who just stood there and looked at him. Finally, she said, "Oh, give it to me." She took the knife and proceeded to clean the deer while Cork held one of the rear legs apart to help.

Now, Linda Lofton was no novice at cleaning deer and elk. She did it once or twice each fall. She usually cleaned her own kills and sometimes Cork's, and she was quite proficient at it. Cork never played the macho scene.

That was the only deer they got that week, but the following week, elk season opened, and they got a bull elk about one quarter of a mile from where deer was killed.

They both shot the elk, and Linda tagged it. They were both standing by it, getting ready to work on it. Cork still had his left hand bandaged and in a plastic bag. He stood there with his knife out again, and he looked over at Linda. She had been pulling one of the legs over and stopped, looking up at him. She gave him a look like, why are you just standing there? Get to work. And then she looked at his hand and didn't say a word.

Finally, she said "OK" and held her hand out, and Cork gave her the knife.

Cleaning an elk is not like cleaning a deer. Elk are a lot bigger, and it's more difficult. It takes quite a bit of strength, and Linda was not a very big person. In fact, just getting the stomach out is quite an achievement, let alone the rest of the process. Cork helped as much as he could with his one good hand.

After the stomach was out, Linda had to almost crawl inside the elk to get at the heart and lungs. Cork was standing behind her as she was doing this, and she was down on both knees and inside the elk, almost up to her midsection. Because she was having trouble cutting and getting loose the lungs, her fanny was wiggling back and forth inside her rain pants, and Cork got tickled at the sight and started laughing out loud. That was not the thing to do.

There was no more wiggling, and very quickly she backed out and stood up facing Cork. She had his knife in one hand, the heart in the other, and blood all over her, and she was totally pissed.

Linda was a little over five feet tall and had blond hair that she usually wore in a ponytail under a hat while hunting, but not right at that moment. She had blood in her hair and blood on her face. Her eyes were half closed, and her teeth were clenched together. Cork thought that was just about the cutest thing he had ever seen in his life and was down on the ground laughing. If looks could kill, Cork would have been in a lot trouble.

She set the knife and heart on the ground and said, "You can finish it." Then she stomped away to clean herself with some wet ferns.

CHAPTER 15

As Cork continued driving toward the Nestucca River, grinning to himself, he wondered what Linda had yelled at him as he drove through the gate. Maybe he didn't really want to know.

He had been going too fast and made himself slow down. It wouldn't help matters at all if he had an accident or got stopped for speeding.

He was worried about Johnathon. He knew how impulsive he could be sometimes—no, a lot of the time. Johnathon would do things or say things without thinking.

A lot of people said that Cork and Johnathon not only looked a lot alike but acted a lot alike also. In fact, some people had mistaken them for brothers.

Cork remembered his son, Wayne Jr., when he was about ten years old, saying "Dad, that man looks just like you" after meeting Johnathon for the first time.

Well, they may have looked a little alike, but they definitely were two different people. At least Cork thought so. People had started calling Johnathon Old Man in recent years, and he didn't like that very much. That was probably why they did it. Nobody called Cork Old Man. Not that he would mind. Heck, after being called Cork or Corky all his life, Old Man would probably be a welcome change.

Cork had even started calling Johnathon Old Man sometimes, and they were about the same age.

Lucy and Linda were close in age too, but Cork thought Lucy was a couple of years older.

While Cork was driving back, he kept browbeating himself. If Johnathon got hurt while Cork was gone, he would never forgive himself. He should have called Linda before he left. Christ, he would still have the boat with him to help Johnathon. Now there would be no way to follow the fish if it decided to go back downstream. Of course, if the fish decided to go upstream, it wouldn't have made any difference. There was no way to get the drift boat upstream over those riffles. Bringing the boat back now was not an option, he would have had to launch the drift boat up river from Johnathon and take the time to drift down river to him.

Cork still had his doubts that they could ever get the fish to the bank. He had never seen a salmon that big, if that was what it really was. If in fact it was a salmon, it would have to be a world-record salmon. He had seen some awfully big Chinook salmon when he lived in Alaska, but he had never seen one as big as the fish that Johnathon had on his line. The biggest one that he was aware of was caught commercially in Petersburg, Alaska, some time ago, and it was around 125 pounds. The biggest one that Cork had seen in person was just over 70 pounds, and the fish that Cork had seen that day was a lot bigger than that.

He wondered why a fish that big would be in the Nestucca River. An Alaskan river, maybe, but not a river in the lower forty-eight. He remembered seeing some big Chinooks caught in the Tillamook Bay area back in the nineteen seventies, and he had seen one that weighed in at 68 pounds. He had even heard of some caught that were bigger. He in fact had caught one in the Trask River that weighed 59 pounds, the biggest Chinook that he had ever caught.

Of course, Johnathon had told Cork that he had caught one that weighed 61 pounds, but he was smiling when he said it, and Cork didn't know whether to believe him. Johnathon was always trying to outdo Cork, whether it was a fact or not.

He had heard that the fish and Game Commission of Oregon had obtained some salmon eggs or breeding stock from a hatchery on the Kenai River in Alaska during that time and had somehow crossbred or allowed the strain to develop in the Trask River Hatchery, and that was the reason for the big fish in Tillamook Bay during those years. Of course, that was just a rumor.

He had heard of no such rumor to explain why a Chinook salmon that big would be coming up the Nestucca River to spawn, if in fact it was a Chinook.

As Cork was driving and thinking back to when he had seen the fish in the riffle, he just shook his head and thought, "No, that couldn't be a Salmon. That fish was bigger than a large seal, quite a bit bigger."

He hoped that Johnathon would still have the fish on when he got there and that they could see what it really was before it came off the hook.

Johnathon had told Cork that he had had the fish on for over two hours when Cork had come up to him on the river, and Cork figured that he had been gone for around two hours and wouldn't get there for another hour because he still had to walk downriver for a quarter of a mile after parking his vehicle.

Wow, that was a long time. He had doubts that Johnathon would still have the fish on. The hook in the fish's jaw would eventually enlarge the hole and fall out with the help of a little slack line. A fisherman can keep applying constant tight line for only so long, especially an older person. Cork had seen that happen many times, even to himself. Sometimes when a fisherman is landing a fish with a dip net, the hook falls out because the line goes slack in the process.

CHAPTER 16

Johnathon was in pretty good physical condition for a man his age. He exercised every morning, like Cork did, unless he had to leave the house early to go hunting or fishing. When that happened, he would just do some stretches and go out the door.

He had gone to Vietnam in the army, just out of high school—a decision he regretted the rest of his life.

He always said it wasn't going into the army that was a bad move; it was going to Vietnam. Of course, that wasn't his choice. There was nothing he could do about it. Once you were in the army, you went where they told you to go.

He was in Asia for two years, sometimes under fire and sometimes not. He saw and did some things that he wished he could totally forget, but, of course, that was impossible.

He became a sergeant in the infantry after the first year, and he learned not to make close friends after a mortar killed three of his closest friends. One died in his hands as he knelt beside him. His name was Joseph, and Johnathon went off by himself and wept for an hour.

They had all been playing cards in a bunker, and Johnathon had gone outside to the head to relieve himself when it blew up. It took a direct hit, and after that he always thought he had been saved by the powers above for something that would happen in his future life. But for the life of him, he never could figure out what that would be, because he didn't figure he was exceptional in anything.

He believed in God, but he wasn't overly religious. He had been to church many times as a kid growing up but wasn't a regular, so he didn't think what he was being saved for had anything to do with religion.

He was wounded twice, once in the right arm and once in the left leg, neither of which hit a bone, and he recovered fast and was returned to combat. This also enforced the idea that he was being saved for something.

The rest of his platoon picked up on it as well. Some of them looked at him out of the corners of their eyes and treated him with awe, while others teased him and pointed at him and would bow down sometimes in jest.

But, one thing for sure, they all wanted to stay in Johnathon's platoon. They liked and trusted him as their platoon leader and figured he had saved their bacon more than once.

One time, Johnathon was leading his men down a road outside a small village when he noticed a young child running at them. He yelled "Down!" when he saw the child was carrying what looked like a grenade in both hands.

He immediately shot with his rifle without thinking and hit the child in the chest, slamming the child backward, and the grenade went off. No soldier in the platoon was injured, but since Johnathon was the closest and the only one left standing when it went off, the explosion threw him back a good twenty feet.

Again, he was not injured. This just added to his reputation, and every soldier in his company heard about him and wanted in his platoon when there was a vacancy. But there never was one.

The bad thing about this was that his company commander heard the gossip and rumors and had a tendency to send Johnathon and his platoon into some of the most dangerous situations. Not to be mean or anything like that, but just because he figured Johnathon could complete his mission without getting anybody injured. And he was right. Very few of the soldiers in Johnathon's platoon ever got hurt, and none lost their lives during the time he was their platoon leader, up to the time he rotated back to the States.

The army tried to get him to reenlist, but he would have nothing to do with it. He told them he had to go home and catch some salmon.

Johnathon never got over the child he shot. He knew that he had done the right thing, and if he hadn't have done it, he and his platoon would have been killed. But he couldn't forget the look on that child's face as he or she—he didn't know which—ran toward him and his platoon. It was pure hate, absolutely pure hate.

Many times, he would have a nightmare involving this incident and wake up Lucy with his screaming. When she asked what it was all about, he wouldn't tell her, and he never did. He would just say it was about the war and leave it at that. But he did tell Cork. He knew that he would understand, and he did.

It happened one day while they were salmon fishing in Johnathon's boat. It was a beautiful day; the weather was great, but the fishing was lousy. They had already been on the river for about four hours and had only one bite, with no fish in the boat.

They were sitting in the lower part of the 101 hole, anchored up with divers and eggs out. It was around lunchtime, so they were eating their sandwiches, and Cork was talking about how things in life were so unpredictable.

He was telling Johnathon that when he was a traffic officer in the Oregon State Police, before he transferred to Game Division, he had stopped a young lady for speeding, just within the city limits of Astoria.

He was writing a citation, and since there was so much noise coming from cars on the highway, he was bent over trying to hear what the lady was saying and took his eyes off the traffic.

A pickup coming up in one of two northbound lanes swerved over and hit him. The vehicle was estimated to be going around fifty miles per hour, and it happened so fast that Cork tried but couldn't get out of the way in time.

The force of impact made Cork spin up the side of the lady's car, leaving boot polish on her door, taking off her side rearview mirror, and knocking him fifty-two feet through the air before he came down in the front yard of a house.

He momentarily lost consciousness while in the air and came to attempting to crawl to his patrol car.

Several drivers witnessed the accident and came to a screeching halt on the highway, coming to Cork's aid.

An ambulance came to take Cork to the hospital, and the driver of the pickup truck, who had stopped approximately two blocks down the highway, was arrested by the Astoria City Police for drunk driving.

Cork was lying on an emergency room examination table with three doctors and four nurses in attendance cutting his uniform off him and checking the extent of his injuries when in ran Helen, Cork's wife at the time.

She ran right up to Cork, and, instead of inquiring about his condition, said in a loud voice that everyone in the room could hear, "Oh, Cork, I bet you didn't change your underwear this morning."

The mood in the emergency room up until this time had been very solemn. Not only was there extensive trauma to Cork's right upper leg, but internal injuries and bleeding were also suspected.

When Cork's wife uttered her concern, the change of mood was quite evident. Everyone in the room was showing signs of hysteria—apart from Cork, who was still in shock from the accident and not in the mood for any humor of this sort.

As it turned out, Cork's injuries were not as serious as the doctors expected, due to Cork's age and good physical condition. One doctor told Cork that if he had been ten years older, he probably would not have survived. Cork went back to work two months later.

Johnathon, hearing what Cork's wife said at the hospital, was laughing out loud when Cork, with a rather solemn look on his face, said, "Johnathon, it wasn't that funny at the time."

Johnathon said, "Maybe not at the time, but it sure sounds funny the way you just told it. Is that the reason you split from her?"

Cork looked at him for a second and then said, "For Christ's sake, no. And I would appreciate it if you would quit laughing so damned loud."

He then added, "And, by the way, I take a shower and change my underwear every morning, and she knew that." He was grinning. "I don't know why she said that. Just being humorous, I guess."

CHAPTER 17

That was when Johnathon told Cork about the incident in Vietnam involving the child. He told him the whole story—some things that he had never told anyone else, and even some things that he hadn't even remembered until then.

During the last five minutes or so of the story, Johnathon had tears running down his cheeks and dripping off his chin. His voice was shaking and lower lip quivering, and Cork's heart went out to him.

Cork had been standing up with his fishing pole in his hands, and Johnathon was sitting down with his head down, telling the story. Cork laid his pole down and put his right hand on Johnathon's left shoulder.

He didn't say anything for a good minute, and then he said, "It's OK, John." In fact, he didn't know what to say. He was thinking, what do you say to a friend who has just told you the worst nightmare of his life?

Finally, Cork told Johnathon, "I'm sure you've been told that you're a hero for saving your life and the lives of your men, and that would be true. You're a hero for sure, but did you ever think that the child who was killed was just as much a soldier as any person who was twice or three times his age and wearing a uniform? The person carrying that grenade was trained to use it to kill. It made no difference what age they were."

Cork said, "Johnathon, if you had not pulled the trigger on your weapon as soon as you did and the person had gotten closer to you and your platoon before it went off, the result would have been horrific. You would have blamed yourself for not shooting, and I would think that would have been a worse thing to live with, if you in fact lived through it."

Cork went on to say that there was no doubt that he had witnessed and been involved in many bad and unsightly situations in Vietnam while he was there. That is what war is like.

He stopped talking for a minute. Johnathon was quiet and calming down somewhat.

Cork said, "John, I was never in the war, as you know, but I've seen things in my life that I don't like to think about, let alone talk about."

When Cork was growing up, his dad was a police officer and told Cork many things that he had witnessed. But it was nothing like experiencing them in person, as he did in the Coast Guard and when he was a police officer himself.

Cork told Johnathon about being in the Coast Guard and stationed in Alaska during the earthquake and tidal wave of 1964, when he was a young man. There were several incidents during that time, when he was nineteen years old, that hardened him somewhat. The worst was probably picking up bodies from the ocean that had been picked and eaten by the seagulls. Cork was on lookout duty on the bridge of the ship he was stationed on when he spotted a whole group of seagulls sitting on something that was bobbing up and down in the water. He told the officer on deck, and upon closer inspection, they found it to be a human body killed by the tidal wave.

He told Johnathon that it was the first time he had ever encountered a dead person killed in the outdoors, and he had never forgotten it, although he had seen many since, and some a lot worse, such as a few killed and eaten by bears in Alaska.

Cork said one of the hardest parts of being a police officer is to inform relatives of a person who has been killed by some accident or animal that they have lost a child, husband, wife, mother, or father. He said that it was totally heart wrenching, and most officers couldn't hold the tears back. He added that it was something he never volunteered for.

Johnathon and Cork had been close friends up to this time, but the disclosure of some of the bad moments in their lives made them closer. Their friends and family could tell the difference and even inquired about it.

Linda asked Cork if something had happened between the two one time, saying that they were acting a little different. She said she couldn't put her finger on it; it was just that they weren't clowning around as much as they used to. They were acting more mature or something.

Cork just looked at her and said, "Oh, good grief, Linda. It's probably that John told me a few things about himself in his early years."

Linda asked, "Is it something I would be interested in?"

Cork turned to her and said, "No, definitely not," and he gave her a rather stern look. She never asked again.

CHAPTER 18

When a person is going through a certain amount of stress, such as Cork was while driving back to the Nestucca River that day, many things go through his or her mind.

He had about a half hour of driving time before he'd reach Hebo and a little more time to reach Johnathon on the river. He knew that if anything had happened to Johnathon while he was gone, like a heart attack, or if he injured himself while fighting that damned fish, Cork was going to blame himself.

He had been cussing himself out loud for the last half hour. He knew it wouldn't do any good, but it let him get out a little frustration. He was at the point of tears several times, and that just made him madder at himself.

He had just gone over the summit of the Coast Range on Highway 22 when he came around a sharp corner to the right a little too fast because he was thinking about

Johnathon and not paying attention to his speed, and he met a cow elk all by herself, standing in his lane.

When something like this happens to a person, a momentarily shock that brings him back to reality, it seems like time stands still, which was how Cork felt at that moment.

Cork, who was traveling at about forty-five miles per hour—not fast but still too fast for that corner—never hit his brakes but jerked the steering wheel to the right, just barely touching the elk and keeping his right front wheel on the two-foot gravel shoulder.

Cork felt a thump on the pickup and heard a noise as he breezed by the elk, but he didn't have time to worry about it because the vehicle was now out of control, sliding around the corner sideways.

Still sideways in the road, halfway across the center line and still going, probably, forty miles per hour, Cork looked over and saw a fully loaded log truck coming at him in the opposite lane.

Cork whipped the wheel to the left and slammed on the gas. The pickup's rear end slid around into his lane just as the logging truck went by.

Cork could see the truck driver's face as he went by. His eyes were as big as saucers. There was absolutely nothing the truck driver could do but hold on to the steering wheel and hit his brakes, which he did. There was virtually no shoulder on that side of the highway and a steep bank down into the canyon.

Thankfully, the truck driver didn't lose control and made it around the corner. Cork, looking through his rearview mirror, saw him keep going amid all the blue smoke in the air from the truck's tires.

He hoped the elk had gotten off the highway before the truck came around the corner; otherwise, there was going to be a real mess to clean up.

Down the road about one hundred yards was a gravel pullout, and Cork used it. He stopped, turned the engine off, and sat there, leaning forward on the steering wheel and trying to collect his thoughts and calm down.

Cork had been through a lot of close calls in his life. He figured it just wasn't his time yet, but his luck had to run out sometime.

He finally got out of the pickup, on shaky legs, and checked for any damage. The tires were full and OK, but he remembered hearing a thump when he went by the elk. Checking the left side of the vehicle, he found a large dent in his driver door.

Looking closer, he figured it out. The elk had been startled, of course, and had kicked backward, striking his door with its hind foot. He said out loud, "Damn. That elk cost me about four hundred dollars." And then he thought, I guess that's cheap. It could have been my life.

Cork got back into his pickup, turned around, and drove back up the highway. He wanted to see if the truck had hit the elk around the bend. He hadn't see it in his rearview mirror.

When he got back to the area where the elk was, he slowed down so he could see over the bank. There was no evidence of the elk, dead or alive, so he figured the elk, after being so startled and kicking his door, had immediately jumped over the bank and run off.

He went up the road, turned around, and headed back toward Hebo and Johnathon. Cork was using some rather profane words and thinking, what else is going to happen before I get back to the river?

Finally reaching Hebo, he stopped at the sporting goods store. Leaving his vehicle running, he ran into the store to buy a can of pop.

Patrick, the owner, wanted to know where he was headed so fast. Cork told him that he had left Johnathon on the river fighting a big fish, and he had to get back to him.

Pat said, "Hell, Cork, I seen you drive by here, going like the dickens and pulling your boat over an hour ago and not stopping like you usually do. I wondered what was going on."

Cork, without stopping to pay for the pop, said that he would be back as soon as possible and tell him all about it. He jumped into his pickup and took off too fast, spilling his can of pop down the front of his coat.

As he put the can in the cup holder on the dash and brushed the liquid of his coat, he thought, this is turning into one hell of a day; that's for sure.

The fish

CHAPTER 19

THE FISH

The fish is indeed a Chinook salmon. In different parts of the country it goes by different names, such as King Salmon, Quinnat, Tule, Tyee, Black Mouth, and various others, but on the Nestucca River, it's called Chinook.

It is one of the major sources of food, along with the other four species of salmon in the Pacific Northwest, and it has been since the existence of humans.

The Native Americans along the Pacific Ocean have legends and stories handed down for generations pertaining to the Chinook salmon. It can be said that the species held a significant place in their culture, and some tribes are named Chinook, after the fish.

The question is, What came first—humans or the salmon? The consensus is the salmon.

Of the five Pacific salmon, the Chinook is the largest but also the least abundant.

The largest Chinook salmon on record was commercially caught in Alaska and was around 126 pounds. The largest one caught by a sport fisherman was 97 pounds and was also from Alaska.

There were no records taken or kept prior to the middle twentieth century, so to say no one ever caught a Chinook salmon bigger than that would be a fallacy.

There are Indian legends pertaining to enormous salmon; they may be fact or fiction.

The Chinook salmon is one of the most magnificent and beautiful creatures on God's earth. From juvenile to spawning maturity, they are silver in color with a bluish-black back that when observed in the ocean or in rivers, swimming or in pursuit of prey, give off a magnificent and brilliant flash that can be seen for some distance.

When hooked, the Chinook generally stays deep, although it does come out of the water sometimes when hooked in the body instead of the mouth.

When a sports fisherman is fighting one of these large fish and observes the flash down deep in the water, whether ocean or river, it makes the fish seem much larger than it is. Usually there is a verbal exclamation such as "Oh, my God" or something similar and a sudden urge to relieve his bodily functions. It is an experience not soon forgotten. The fish in this story, as stated earlier, is a Chinook salmon, but what a salmon. It is a throwback to earlier days and a size that would be totally unbelievable—quite a bit bigger than anything on record, with a weight close to two hundred pounds.

That's not to say a fish that size has not been hooked by a sport or commercial fisherman sometime in the last century. But if it was, it was not landed or recorded.

There have been many stories from sport and commercial fishermen of hooking a fish that never stopped and was never seen. In most cases the gear that was used to hook the fish was lost also, in its entirety, so who is to say that it wasn't a monster Chinook salmon?

CHAPTER 20

Approximately ten years prior to Johnathon and Cork's encounter with the fish, during the same time of year, give or take a couple of weeks, a female hen Chinook salmon was swimming, or shall we say cruising, with several other salmon around the mouth of the Nestucca River in the Pacific Ocean.

Salmon never lie still. They are generally always moving. When they seem to be staying in one place, they are usually in a slight current, and by using their numerous fins and tail, they appear to be motionless.

The salmon was big, even for her species, probably in the neighborhood of fifty pounds, and was in prime condition.

She had been cruising the Pacific Ocean for over five years, and she was ready to come home to her river of birth and spawn with the help of a mate of her choosing.

She was still eating as much as she could but probably knew that she would soon stop. Chinook salmon, once they enter freshwater on their spawning run, discontinue consuming food but continue by living off the body fat or protein they've built up. Whether a salmon has knowledge of this or not is unknown. What is known is they feed a lot before entering freshwater. And generally, along the Pacific Coast during this time of year, there is no shortage of food for the salmon.

She probably had regurgitated some of her food intake by now, so she knew change was coming and that the eggs she had been carrying for quite some time were getting larger in her stomach and changing her swimming habits by slowing her down to a small degree.

She knew exactly where she had to go. Every time she approached where the Nestucca River's water entered the Pacific, she could smell the freshwater that was mixed with the salty brine, and she instinctively knew that was her destination and had been for some time.

The pull was great, but she didn't feel ready yet. Whether it was because the water temperature was still too warm or her body was telling her it wasn't ready, she kept turning from entering the river and continued swimming in a large arc in the ocean.

She did notice that the fish population was increasing near the portion of the Pacific that she was traveling. More of her kind apparently were feeling the urge to travel back to their birth river.

Also, she noticed the area near the mouth of the river was getting crowded with predators, some of the ones she had been running from and dodging all her life. She could usually outswim the big brown ones if she was in an uncrowded and open area, but she also knew that confinement like the mouth of the river would lessen the chances of escape.

Every time she came near the inlet, she could smell blood and death in the water and knew that the chance of getting through the gauntlet and up into the river was almost nil. Many of her kind were not making it.

She also noticed many large shadows in the water and on the bottom near the mouth of the river and observed many of her kind thrashing and making noise near these shadows. She didn't really understand, but it did cause her to avoid them as much as possible, which was rather hard to do since they were covering the surface.

She saw a lot of small fish in and near the mouth of the river, some near the shadows—fish that she was accustomed to feeding on, but she always turned away.

One time she didn't turn away and went for one of the small fish, which was acting as if it was injured. She was traveling slowly and watching the fish as she approached, but just as she grabbed it in her mouth, she noticed one of the large brown predators coming fast toward her.

She immediately burst forth with all her power and speed.

As she headed directly out into the ocean, away from the mouth of the river, she felt a pain and pressure in the upper part of her mouth. This just added to the fright of the brown thing coming after her, and she shot like a fifty-pound silver bullet out into the deep part of the ocean.

Nothing could have stopped her, and definitely not the hook and the thirty yards of fishing line attached to the pole, reel, and pole holder as she pulled it through the surf. All of which came from a sixteen-foot sport fishing boat with two men standing up in it and screaming very loudly, just inside the surf line.

After traveling some distance and leaving the seal out of sight behind her, she started to slow, and, in doing so, she shook her head violently back and forth, opening and closing her mouth, dislodging the hook.

Of course, she didn't know what it was, but the pain and pressure were gone, and that was all she cared about.

She had spent her entire life doing just that—getting rid of something in her mouth that she didn't like the taste of or something that had gotten stuck or was causing her some sort of pain. In other words, something that she didn't want to swallow.

She, like all other salmon, had spent her entire life doing nothing but swimming and eating anything that appeared edible. And she was exceptionally good at it. That was the reason she had reached the size she was.

She had learned to swim fast and deep when something was after her or when she was scared, and that was where she was when she slowed down and threw the hook and line out of her mouth—very deep in the ocean. It had been her home for most of her life, and she knew exactly where she was.

She encountered a couple of schools of herring on the way back up and grabbed a couple of them out of habit. She wasn't hungry. One of the little fish wouldn't stay down, and she threw it back out. That had been happening more frequently as of late. She didn't really know why, but it didn't concern her.

When she got back closer to landfall, she was a few miles south of the Nestucca due to the current that pushed south in the ocean. It didn't bother her. She could smell the river water in the ocean, and she headed back into it.

Time was getting closer now. She could feel the change in her body, and the drive to move into freshwater was becoming more prominent. She was reluctant to get to close to the inlet due to her last experience, but she knew the time was coming when there was not going to be any alternative.

CHAPTER 21

After a couple of days, the big female Chinook could feel and smell a change in the river water that was mixed with the ocean water. It was colder and had sediment mixed in with it. In other words, it had a muddy content.

The drive in her now became uncontrollable. She had to go. She entered the river inlet.

From that point forward, she would consume no more food. Her body would not permit it. For the rest of her life, she would live off stored fat and protein.

This is not to say she was not going to try. The feeding instinct was just too great. Her number-one drive all her life had been to eat, and that would not change immediately. She would continue to take different things into her mouth that she thought or knew were food. But she would not or could not swallow them and would eventually spit them back out.

Her sole drive and purpose now was to swim up the river of her birth and spawn like all her ancestors. This she would accomplish unless she was blocked by some dam or obstacle—at that time there were none on the Nestucca—or by losing her life to a predator, of which there were plenty, humans being the worst, of course, but seals came in a close second. In tidewater, seals are worse because they prey on the upstream migrants day and night, and not only just for food. Seals, not unlike a cat or coyote, like to chase and kill for the sheer enjoyment.

When they kill, they very seldom eat the entire fish unless it is very small. Generally, they eat the choice parts, such as the belly and eggs, and leave the rest to be consumed by crabs, seagulls, and other scavengers.

The truth is that a very small percentage of salmon that are hatched in the wild ever return, due to all the obstacles they must overcome. The female Chinook in this story just happens to be one of them.

It had been raining for about two days on the Oregon coast and mountains when she entered the Nestucca River system. The river had risen, and the freshwater content of the tidal area had increased, although the water was still brackish due to the proximity to the ocean.

By chance it was night, which made it difficult for predators to see her. It didn't help with seals, of course, and she could hear thrashing and splashing all around her as she traveled up the deepest channel that she could find. The smell of death and blood was quite prevalent now and then, but she didn't stop or turn back.

After traveling about two miles, she came to a deeper spot in the river. The rushing water was a little less turbulent near the bottom, so she decided to stop and rest. She could sense that others of her kind were near her and occasionally could feel one brush up next to her, but the water was to murky to see far.

The water current increased, so she moved to the head of the deeper area, where it started to shallow up again. It became less brackish, and she could tell the difference but not the reason why. In fact, the tide had changed and was heading out, taking a lot of the ocean water with it.

The freshwater did not bother her physically or disable her in any way. Chinook salmon can live and sustain in either freshwater or saltwater. She could tell the difference, though, and changing from one to the other quickly would most likely take some getting used to.

Salmon develop a slime or coating on their bodies after they enter freshwater, and it stays with them until they spawn. At first it's slightly white in color and can be removed easily, but as the salmon ages, it becomes clearer and very sticky.

Some of the salmon that came up into the lower part of the river and bay system with the high tide turned and went back down. Apparently they didn't have the drive to continue, as our female did. They probably weren't as mature.

She pushed over the next shallow area and found another deep spot, as big as the first. The water was still brackish but was getting fresher all the time, so she decided to hold for a time.

The brown predators were still present but passed through, heading back downriver. She sensed this more than observed it.

There was a lot splashing on the river's surface, and many different-colored objects were passing through. She had never observed these attractive things before and had the urge to chase one and strike it but didn't.

Although visibility was limited due to the muddy water, not only could she see the wiggling, many-colored objects, but she also saw and smelled eggs from her own kind floating in the tidal current. The eggs were usually accompanied by a small crawling creature that she remembered from her past when she was in the estuary as a juvenile. She remembered eating them then.

All these things brought out the feeding instinct in her, but she was too nervous from all the new surroundings and noises to do that. Besides, she wasn't hungry anyway.

One time she started out after a small bunch of eggs, but before she could grab them, one of the colored shining objects splashed in front of her. And as she ducked under it to get the eggs, it stung her back, just in front of her big fin. She shook it loose, but the pain scared her and sent her back to the deep spot where she had been resting.

CHAPTER 22

Unbeknown to the female Chinook, she had stopped at one of the most popular fishing holes on the lower river, the Boat Ramp Hole. The tide had turned and was about halfway out. There were approximately fifty people fishing from the bank on the west side and from the five or six boats on the east side.

This was not an unusual number of fishermen at this particular spot during the fall months when the salmon were running. Some days there were more, depending on many conditions, such as the tide change and amount; the weather; and the water condition, clarity, and river height due to the fall rains.

They usually cast spinners or wobblers, all different sizes, shapes, and colors. Also, they used bobbers with salmon eggs and sand shrimp as bait. Both methods are highly effective when fish are biting, which is not all the time.

Several fish are foul hooked, whether intentional or accidental, during certain times when there are a lot in the river. It has created a problem for the Oregon State Fish and Game Commission and the Oregon State Police over the years because fish can only be taken legally when hooked in the mouth. When fish are not hooked in the mouth they are usually snagged. Snagging causes damage to the fish and the sustainability of the fishery. Most fishermen do not intentionally try to snag or foul hook a fish, but there are always a few, which makes it hard on everyone.

One thing about the Boat Ramp Hole—there are usually so many anglers present that if a fish comes in foul hooked, it is usually released unharmed due to the presence of so many people. They tend to police themselves. In other words, it is never known who is standing next to the person landing an illegally hooked fish. It could be a game officer, and the fines and penalties are high.

The Boat Ramp Hole is only one of many holes on the Nestucca River that the fish tend to hold up in, but it is one of the first for the fish coming out of the ocean. Here the fish are usually still bright and have salmon lice—or, as they're commonly called, sea lice—behind their anal fin, which means they're fresh.

Sea lice are parasites that attach themselves to the fish in saltwater but drop off after the fish has been in freshwater after a certain amount of time. They don't drop off all at once but gradually, as the salmon move up the river. They will usually be all gone after approximately two weeks, leaving telltale marks or scars behind the anal fin, the first fin in front of the tail on the bottom or belly of the fish.

Sea lice sometimes attach themselves to the gills and other parts of a salmon's body, and although they do feed off the blood of the fish, little harm is done when they're in small numbers. In large numbers—if the fish is saturated with them—death can occur from open wounds caused by the sea lice because bacteria and disease can enter.

The female Chinook of our story, just arriving in freshwater, coming out of the ocean, had ten to twenty sea lice attached to her. Whether they caused her any pain or hindrance is unknown, although it wouldn't be out of the question to believe she might have some type of irritation from them. When a Chinook salmon jumps out of the water on its way up the river, one theory is that it is trying to shake off these sea lice. Whether this is true or not is unknown.

Regardless of the sea lice, our female Chinook is in prime condition, with no injuries or scars from seal bites. She is strong and ready to run the gauntlet up the Nestucca River to her birthplace on Moon Creek, which is approximately twenty miles away.

Besides the seals in the lower river and the multitude of fishermen throughout the entire river system, there were other predators and hazardous conditions to confront.

Otters, which are in abundance on the Nestucca River, are deadly, especially when they are hunting in a pack or group, which consists of a large family. They generally prey upon small fish, insects, clams, and small crustaceans, or just about anything they can eat. But they will attack a salmon, especially if they get it cornered in shallow water or find one that is hurt and can't get away from them.

It is not unusual for a boater to observe an otter or a group of otters feeding on a salmon in the upper tidewater area below the town of Cloverdale on the Nestucca.

The weather is a major factor for our female Chinook salmon to contend with. In the Coastal Mountains, in Oregon, during the fall months, it tends to rain, and sometimes rain a lot. This affects the water level of the river, and there are also mudslides, windblown trees, and other obstacles the fish must travel through or around on their way upstream.

In a good year, the first rains come in late September or the first of October and are moderate. The river level fluctuates from approximately three and a half feet to six feet above normal flow. It's not so low that it would hamper the fish going over the numerous riffles and not so high as to constitute flooding over the banks and into farm fields. A lot of debris—leaves, tree limbs, and such—comes down the river during this first rain. It's like Mother Earth is cleaning herself, although the salmon have no trouble traversing up the river.

If it rained on and off, once or twice a week during October and November, and the river didn't flood or have a drought and drop to low, the fish should have no problem reaching their destinations and be in good condition to complete their spawning process.

In a bad year, the river can stay at the low summer level, with hardly enough water for the salmon to make it over some of the riffles. In some cases, salmon have had to spawn in the middle or lower part of the river. This would probably be sufficient except that if heavy rains in late December caused floodwater, heavy with silt and mud, it could damage the redds (salmon spawning beds), leaving them open to predation and/or covering them with mud, which would suffocate the eggs.

Also, an excessive amount of floodwater can be detrimental to the spawning salmon. When the rains are so heavy through the months of October and November that the river is in constant flood stage, salmon sometimes make the wrong turn and end up in farm fields, highway ditches, and various other places—none of which is good spawning habitat.

CHAPTER 23

On the next high tide, the female Chinook, feeling the change in water flow and with the increase of salt in the water, decided to move upstream.

She was not in that big a hurry. She had the unmistakable urge, but she also knew it was not time yet. Possibly like a woman in her seventh month of pregnancy, she was showing with a growing infant in her womb, but she knew that there was still some time before giving birth and continued with her daily life.

The female Chinook, like the woman, knew the time was coming. She could feel the change in her body, and she knew she was in the right place—her birth river—but she also knew that it was not time yet. So there was no real hurry. Otherwise, she would blast up the river like a rocket and not stop until her destination was reached.

She traveled as much as a mile upstream, until she reached another deep hole in the river and felt and smelled more freshwater. The river, still a little murky from the rain a few days prior, was clearing and dropping in depth.

This spot in the river was calmer but more confined. She was not as nervous.

She didn't see or sense any of the brown things that had been chasing her kind since she had entered the river.

Our female Chinook, not in any hurry to leave, stayed for some time.

She found a downed log lying in the river up against a rocky bank, and she found a place in the water, under the log, big enough for her to lie hidden and suspended. This was good, and she liked it—nothing was bothering her. She came out periodically and swam around the hole, came to the surface and jumped, and then went back to her hiding spot.

She saw many other creatures in the river while waiting—bottom dwellers that crawled around in the mud; many other fish, including salmon like her; and birds that dived deep to catch small fish.

She caught some of the small fish like she used to, to eat. But they wouldn't go down, and she spit them back out. She really wasn't hungry anyway.

Within a couple of weeks, it rained. Smelling and tasting the freshwater as the river rose, she decided to move on up.

She left during the hours of darkness and didn't stop until just before daylight. She had totally left all evidence of the tidal influence and brackish water. Although she was swimming in slightly muddy water, it was all fresh.

She distinctly smelled the water that she was born in, which was a small tributary of the main river. The smell was much clearer now, and it made her want to continue. But she didn't. She holed up in a reasonably deep area with fast-running water.

The area that she was in was only about five feet deep, but with the muddy color of the water, she was totally concealed. The only bad thing about it was that she must be moving continuously. That burned energy, and, consequently, protein and fat, which she had a limited supply of.

She had no knowledge of this, of course, but she must have realized that she couldn't move as fast as she once could, and she tired more easily. Also, her eggs were maturing and using up a lot of her protein.

The female Chinook had been in the river about three weeks now. She was not the silver, sleek, and streamlined creature that she had been coming out of the ocean. She was still silver in some spots, but gray and even black in others. There was white showing on the bottom part of her tail, probably from swimming so close to the bottom of the river and rubbing on the rocks.

She was wearing down and had a gaunt look from using up her body's reserves.

The rain had kept the river at a moderately high stage, perfect for fish to migrate up the river. She felt that it was time to complete her journey, and she started steadily moving.

She kept moving day and night, not stopping until she lost the scent she had been following. She stopped, confused, and turned back down the river. When she finally reached the scent, she again turned back upriver into the current. This time she stayed with it and found that it predominantly flowed down the left side of the river, so she moved up that side instead of the middle, as she had done previously.

Our female Chinook finally reached the tributary flowing in from left side of the river that she remembered and remembered well. She didn't turn directly up it but slowed and stopped just off the mouth. It wasn't very deep here, and it was quite swift. And the water coming out of the small creek was faster flowing yet.

Of course, she didn't know it, but the name of this creek was Moon Creek. It flowed into the Nestucca at a junction in the road called Blaine.

Chinook salmon generally prefer bigger water to spawn in, such as the main stem of the Nestucca, but for some reason of their own, some Chinook spawn up the many small tributaries. This is not something new; it has probably always been that way.

She decided to wait for a while before heading up the creek. The water was dropping, and by instinct, she didn't want to be trapped or stranded in the shallow water. So she drifted downriver for a short distance to a deeper channel. She was still in the flow and scent of the creek, and she still had time before she must release her eggs, so there was no real hurry yet.

She was lying near the bottom keeping up with the current when something slammed into her stomach on the right side. She shot forward and then made a tight circle. As she came around, she noticed one of her kind, but smaller, making a pass at her again.

It was a male Chinook salmon, about half the size of our female, and it was hitting her, trying to get her to release eggs although they were not near a red, or spawning bed.

She outdistanced him and then made another tight circle, this time almost coming out of the water and hitting him hard and fast on his left side, knocking him sideways.

The smaller fish immediately righted himself and circled behind her. He was starting to come for her again when the river erupted. A big fish—a great big fish—came upriver behind him and hit him with such force that it knocked him clear out the water.

When the smaller fish got control of himself again, he took off fast upriver and was gone from sight, not to return.

The big fish that had entered the area was a large male Chinook, almost as big or bigger than our female. And if she had lost her sleek and graceful look, this fish was downright ugly.

His nose was hooked down over his lower jaw, almost to the point that it couldn't close. He was all brown and black, with a brilliant red strip down each side from the gill plates almost to the tail. He also had white spots on his belly and lower tail from dragging the bottom in shallow water. His back showed a sharp ridge down it from losing so much fat.

He may not have looked very sleek anymore, but he sure looked mean and powerful.

When things calmed down, he moved up beside her on her left side, about two feet away and about halfway back. He never tried to touch her but just lay there finning.

After a little while, he moved up almost parallel to her, stayed for a few minutes, and then drifted back to his former position.

She never tried to force him away. On the contrary, she acted as if he belonged there. Apparently she had found a mate.

Maybe in a fish's world, just maybe, it was love at first sight. After all, he was big and powerful, so he could protect her, like he already had, and he could protect her eggs when she spawned. With his size and the way he looked, he must come from good stock. So she couldn't ask for any better to fertilize her eggs.

Occasionally, she would move over close to him and touch him. He didn't like it at first, but then, after a period, he would do the same to her but very gently.

And then they looked as if they were playing. They would chase each other around and around, coming to the surface and throwing water everywhere.

Apparently, the male looked quite intimidating, because although a multitude of other fish, including salmon, would swim by them, none would stop or hang around.

Sometimes he would chase one for the fun of it, but he really didn't try to catch it. And, of course, it didn't turn around and come back.

The water had been dropping slightly, and then it started to rain again. After a couple of days, the level of the river and creek had come up substantially.

Our female Chinook knew it was time, and she slowly swam up to the mouth of the creek again. The male swam with her, just slightly back and on her left, which was his usual position.

They both entered the creek at the same time. They had to increase speed because the creek was extremely swift, and it was shallow, even with the increased water level.

It is unknown whether the big male had originated from the creek or just followed his mate. More than likely he came from the creek, like the female—and he could even be one of her siblings—because he never hesitated.

The water just flew as both big fish plowed up the creek. They had to travel approximately one hundred feet to get to deeper water, and then they slowed down. No doubt it took some doing to get that far, considering the condition they were in, but they never hesitated or faltered.

Slowly they kept moving. It was daylight, which helped them to maneuver through the brush and limbs in the water. They never came to an obstacle that stopped them, but they did have to detour around a couple of trees that were in the water, which was still quite an undertaking given their size and the size of the creek.

There was not enough water for them to travel side by side as before, in the big river, so the female was always in the lead, and the male always followed. She would put her eggs where she wanted to anyway. He was just there the help her, protect her from other fish, and fertilize the eggs.

Finally, after about a half mile, she stopped on a gravel bar and swam back and forth across it. She continued doing this for quite some time.

She tested the gravel by turning sideways and using her tail to swish the rocks away from different spots. She must have been satisfied, because then she settled down and just finned in the current as the male took his normal place beside her.

There is no way of knowing whether this was the place she was born, years ago, or just appeared to be the right place at that time. Probably, this was the place she, and maybe even the big male, was born. If she could find the right river and creek after this many years, there is no doubt she could find the right spot.

CHAPTER 24

Finally, it was the right time. The water temperature was just right—rather cold, but it wasn't muddy. The place was the right place; the gravel was what she required, not too big and not too small, so the current could filter oxygenated water to the eggs when they were in place.

She moved up to a spot, and, by turning sideways again, she started moving the gravel until she had a slight depression approximately three to five inches deep and a foot or so across—what is known as a "redd." She dropped below it and looked at it, and then, feeling satisfied, she moved up and over the depression and started laying her eggs.

They were large, even for a chinook, about the size of marbles.

She left approximately two thousand, swished gravel over them, moved up about six feet, and repeated the process.

Meanwhile, the male moved up and over the first redd and started fertilizing the eggs with his milt, which was a white milky substance. Hopefully, it would get to all the eggs in the redd, but it didn't always.

The great majority of eggs are lost before hatching, whether from lack of fertilization, predation, lack of oxygen, or fluctuation of water temperature.

Our female Chinook made and spawned in four redds, and the male who was following spread his milt on them, not only once but numerous times until he was finished.

Sometimes a male salmon will seek out another mate after the one he is with has spawned, but not in this case. The big male was done, and he knew it. He was going to stay in the area with our female and try to protect the eggs as long as possible. After all, even if he could, there were not many, if any, other females around that might need a male in the small creek.

The female and male stayed around the redds for as long as their bodies would allow. Finally, the male could last no longer. He was very weak and could hardly hold himself upright in the current. He drifted down the creek very slowly to the riffle directly below the gravel bar, and he lay over on his side. His time had come, and he died.

About five days later, it was our female's turn. She also became too weak to hold herself upright and lay over in the shallows near the gravel bar where her eggs were. She had fulfilled her destiny and done what her species was meant to do.

Her body and the male Chinook's body would dissolve and return to nature, as it was meant to be. Their body proteins would feed a multitude of living organisms in and around the stream where they had spawned, including the young salmon they had produced.

They were very lucky to complete the cycle, because only three or four adult salmon out of the thousands spawned by a Chinook female ever return. The hazards are great.

CHAPTER 25

The eggs from our female Chinook started to hatch about eleven or twelve weeks from the time she placed them in the gravel. They were not much to look at, only small threadlike creatures with eyes attached to a large yolk sack.

The large Chinook salmon that Johnathon Pane had hooked on the Nestucca River was one of these fish, or alevins, as they are called at this stage of life. They're sometimes food for other fish and various insects, if found and caught, and not many survive this period.

The alevins will stay in the redds until they've absorbed their yolk sac. Then they will work their way up through the gravel that their mother has placed over them and become free swimming and feeding.

During this time, the little Chinooks are called fry. They are ferocious feeders, and our little Chinook was one of the ones out in front. Our fry tried to eat anything it could get in his mouth and swallow. If it moved or wiggled, so much the better.

He was a little bit bigger than its siblings—not much, but there was a noticeable difference. Probably the reason for this was his drive to consume food. Our fry was faster and was the first to get anything eatable; consequently, it was growing at an increasing pace.

The young Chinook learned to hide behind big rocks, stumps, and anywhere that it could see food, largely insects, float by in the current, but where nothing could see it.

There were a lot of close calls that our Chinook had with predators, mainly bigger fish and birds, and he learned to stay out of their way.

Our Chinook moved from the small creek down into the main river with many of the fish that it was born with as the water dropped with the coming summer. The big open water of the Nestucca River was a whole new world for the young fish.

Our Chinook ate anything it could find. It discovered eggs from a late-spawned redd and took as many as he could. Our Chinook was bigger now and chased smaller fish.

During the summer months, our Chinook lived in the deepest holes in the river he could find but gradually moved seaward. His food intake increased because he found more food to eat because of his increase in size.

Sometimes our Chinook went into a feeding frenzy, in which he would eat to the point of gorging and then throw the food back up just to eat some more. This was a habit that he continued when a lot of food was available.

He found that smaller fish were the most satisfying food, and he became efficient at catching and eating any that he could find. He even went after small individuals of his own kind. He didn't know the difference.

He found that farther downstream he traveled, the more food became available.

Our young Chinook fry stopped at three or four miles from the influence of tidewater. It had taken him a long time to get there. He had not been in a hurry and still wasn't.

Where he stopped was a big hole, bigger than any he had been in. It was very deep, and the water was cool. He liked it. There was a lot of food; insects and small fish abounded.

There were also some big fish that attempted to grab him, but he got away.

He still had his parr marks, which are bars and spots along his sides. Most salmon fry have them, but since he was a Chinook, his bar-shaped parr marks were larger than the spaces between them. That is one identifying factor for a Chinook fry. They don't lose them until they get to the brackish water of the lower river.

The parr marks helped our young Chinook hide in the rocks and weeds—kind of a camouflage, if you will.

Our young Chinook stayed in place for almost a year. He was in no hurry to leave, and he was getting bigger and smarter. Finally, after almost doubling in size, he wandered downstream again.

This time he didn't stop until he reached tidewater influence. Here, the water fluctuated from fresh to brackish, depending on the tide.

He hung around this area for some time, confused. His instinct pulled him to continue onward, but it was taking time for him to get used to the saltwater, mentally and physically.

Our young Chinook started to lose his parr marks and developed a dark back, white belly, and silver coloration, which would stay with him most of his life. He was leaving the fry stage and entering his smolt stage. As he moved farther down into the Nestucca estuary, he continued to hunt for food. It seemed that he was always hungry.

He continued to grow and was bigger than almost any salmon his age—in fact, almost twice the size of any of his siblings.

At last he was in the lower bay, close to the ocean. He could tell because the water was almost all saltwater most of the time, with influxes of fresh. Apparently, this occurs when the tide is at low ebb.

Besides the food he had been used to eating the last few months, now there were more morsels to partake of. He found a small crawling creature that came out of the sand bars on high tide, and not only did they have a soft shell and tasted good, they were very nutritious. The best thing about these creatures was that they were very numerous, and he could eat as many as he wanted. And he did!

CHAPTER 26

His instincts finally told him it was time to go out into the ocean. He had adapted to the saltwater, both physically and mentally, by living in the Nestucca Bay for approximately two months.

He had seen numerous members of his kind heading in that direction and not coming back.

The only thing that made him hesitate was that he hated to leave all the food that he had found in the lower bay.

One day, after about three days of rain, when the river was on the rise and a little muddy, he decided to go.

How exhilarating it was for our young Chinook salmon, after being confined in a river and living in freshwater, to enter pure saltwater with all that space to swim and travel in. And another thing—all those creatures swimming and crawling around that he could eat. After all, the main objective in his life was to eat, and he was probably like a kid in a candy store.

He found schools of fish not unlike the ones he used to eat in the rivers, but here there were schools of them swimming together, and they were easy to catch. They tasted a little different, but he really liked them and ate his fill with every bunch he found, although he could only eat the smaller ones for now. Some were just too big to get down, but sometimes he chased them anyway.

He would eventually follow schools of these fish all over the ocean. But for now they didn't seem to be going anywhere, so he just hung around and didn't get too far from them. A lot of his kind were doing the same. There seemed to be salmon everywhere, of all sizes.

There were a lot of predators around also, a lot of the brown ones chasing and eating the bigger salmon. But they didn't chase him much, and when they did go after him, he would swim into a bunch of small fish of his own kind or swim into some seaweed.

One time when he was down near the bottom, hiding in the seaweed, he noticed a small crawly thing almost like the ones he had eaten in the bay water, and he grabbed it. It was good. It had meat in it, unlike the ones in the bay.

When he looked around, he noticed them everywhere, and he ate his fill. Now when the brown things were around trying to catch his brethren, he would come to the bottom, hide in the seaweed, and eat the crawly things.

Now, our young Chinook salmon was not an overly intelligent creature, but even to him this seemed like a good deal. He had figured out a way he could eat all the time and never go hungry. He just kept eating and growing like all good salmon are supposed to do.

He was always bigger than most of the young salmon around him. In fact, always about twice their size. He saw other schools of salmon, adults, more his size, but he had no desire to join them. They were not his siblings or fish his age, and he seemed to know that.

When his group of salmon moved away from the area where the Nestucca River flowed into the ocean, he went with them. It just seemed the right thing to do.

The young salmon always stayed near the bait fish they were feeding on, and when the bait fish left, they either went with them or found another school.

There was never any shortage of crawly things on the bottom to eat, but they preferred little fish.

Occasionally, they would have an encounter with a big fish of huge proportions. Sometimes these big fish would be in groups of three or four. They would move through the schools of salmon fast with their mouths open. They left the smell of blood and death in their path.

When this happened, our young Chinook salmon learned to dive deep. He would go to the bottom and hide if he could. And he found that if the water was too deep, they would not follow. He would wait for some time and then go back up and try to find his group, or what was left of it.

This would happen numerous times during his life in the ocean, no matter where or how far he traveled, which was great.

His school of growing salmon learned early that most predators were near the surface, so they would travel as deep as they could to avoid detection. The only trouble was that the schools or bunches of bait fish that they liked to feed on were always near the surface, which created a real problem.

Of course, they didn't have the intelligence to figure out any strategy, so they tried to travel where the bait fish were and stay down under them. It was easier to do as they got older, bigger, and faster.

For one thing, as the salmon got bigger, the birds that were always after them started leaving them alone, and then, as they got faster, most of them could outswim a brown thing, especially if they headed out into deep water.

Of course, not all of them could. The brown things—seals—instinctively knew which salmon were sick, injured, or just plain slow, and they became a seal's dinner.

Nature has a way of culling out the weakest in any species, and a salmon is no exception.

Our Chinook had nothing to worry about. He was almost twice as big as most any salmon that he was around and always had been. And fast. He could outswim his entire school of fish, which he did, especially when they were after food, eating small fish—herring, sardines, anchovies, and others.

The Chinook salmon of our story just kept eating and getting bigger and bigger.

For the first three or four years at sea, he remained around the school of salmon that he had bunched up with, at first in the mouth of the Nestucca River. But after that, he left. There seemed to be other salmon around all the time, but he didn't stay with any certain group. Instead he just kept swimming and eating.

Two or three times he could smell his home water, the Nestucca, but he had no desire travel any closer. He just kept traveling up and down the Oregon, Washington, and Alaska coasts. Never too close to shore; just staying with or not too far from the bait fish he liked to eat.

Predators didn't bother him much now. He was just too big and fast. He was as big as most of the brown things, and they didn't even try to catch him anymore. Most of the huge fish—killer whales—went after the schools of salmon, not after just one, so he was safe from them. Of course, birds hadn't bothered him for years.

There was one exception. He was leaving the bottom after eating his fill of crawling things—shrimp—when out of nowhere came this huge fish. It came from behind him, and if he hadn't had dove out of reflex, he would have been caught.

It was all white, about four times as big as him, and at first all he could see was teeth.

He went right to the bottom, like he usually did when big fish were around, but that didn't stop this big fish at all. It came right behind him, so he swam into a bunch of seaweed and stayed there.

He swam through the seaweed for some distance, and when he started to come out the other side, *whoosh!* The big fish just missed him, so he turned and went right back in.

To say he was scared would not be correct, because fish probably do not feel that emotion. But they do have enough smarts to avoid danger and try to preserve their lives.

After three or four attempts to leave the seaweed bed and having a close call every time, our Chinook salmon decided to stay put for a while. He noticed a large shadow pass over him a few times, and he knew it was the big fish. He hadn't eaten for some time. He was getting hungry, and he wasn't used to that.

He had gotten a good look at the big fish, and he had seen many like that before—just none that size, and it was fast. It could probably catch him, and he knew it.

He noticed a crawly thing about two feet out in the open, and, without thinking, acting out of pure instinct, he swam out quickly and grabbed it. Seeing a movement coming in his direction, he turned and ducked back into the seaweed when the big fish passed where the crawly thing had been.

The seaweed bed that he was hiding in wasn't very big, and after grabbing the crawly thing, he shot across it and out the other side, straight across an opening and into another bunch of seaweed that covered an enormous area. If he had planned it, which he didn't, he couldn't have planned it any better, because the big fish—a great white shark—was still on the other side looking for him.

He kept traveling in the seaweed but he couldn't go fast like he wanted to so after traveling some distance, he swam above the vegetation and went as fast as he could which he was accustomed to when in danger.

Soon he saw a group of salmon feeding on bait fish and headed directly toward them because he was really hungry now. He was almost to them when a rush of water went by, and something hit him a glancing blow that knocked him to the side.

It was the big fish that had been trailing his scent in the water. Upon seeing the school of salmon, it probably figured a bunch of fish was better than just one fish, so it went past him to attack the group.

Our Chinook salmon immediately changed direction and sped for some distance until he found another school of bait fish. And since he was very hungry now and very tired, he stopped and ate his fill.

CHAPTER 27

Most Chinook salmon return to their stream of origin in three or four years, and some from different areas, mainly Alaska, wait as long as seven years.

Our Chinook was eight years old plus when he finally felt the urge to return to his water of birth. This was probably triggered by the smell of the Nestucca River, which he ran into on his way back north.

At first, he was confused and made a big circle, coming back through the same area he had just traveled. There it was again. There was no mistaking the smell. He felt excited, exhilarated. Probably neither is the right word; let's just say he had a good happy feeling and tried to stay with the smell as he swam. No doubt he recognized the smell of Moon Creek mixed in with the water of the Nestucca.

He had been feeling different for some time, but it didn't bother him. He just kept eating, traveling, and getting bigger. He was a loner. It was safer that way, and he could eat more, which he liked.

It was during the fall months on the Oregon Coast, and, as usual, there had been a lot of rain in the mountains. Consequently, all the rivers were running high, including the Nestucca and all its tributaries. That is probably why our Chinook got a good smell of the river on the outgoing tide.

When he arrived off the mouth of the Nestucca, he wasn't sure what to do. Something urged him to go into the freshwater of the river, but he wasn't sure. Apparently he wasn't feeling the full extent of the need to spawn yet.

He circled offshore for some time, probably close to a week, and the urge became stronger and stronger until he couldn't resist it anymore.

The river was still high from the rain. In fact, there was even more water rushing down the river because the rain hadn't stopped.

He entered the river mouth and headed into the current, which was flowing downstream because the tide was ebbing.

All at once he felt the full effect of the freshwater. He hadn't been in freshwater since he came through these same waters over seven years ago, and it gave him a strange feeling. At first, he almost turned around and headed back out to sea. Then, after a short time, he started to get a longing to proceed on, and he did.

He proceeded slowly; he was in no hurry. He couldn't see well because the water was muddy, but he sensed predators in the area, although nothing was bothering him.

He didn't stop when he left all traces of saltwater. The change rather bothered him, but not to any extreme. He just kept swimming.

After traveling over several shallow areas, he slowed and started to look for a deeper and slower area to stop. It wasn't that he was tired, although he had come a long way. He was still a little confused. He felt that he should be where he was, but he wasn't sure why. He just didn't have that full-blown drive to spawn yet.

Finally, he arrived at a deeper part of the river that he took a liking to. He had to swim over a long, shallow area to get there, but he decided not to travel any farther.

He moved slowly all around the deep area, from side to side and up to the shallower area at the head. It was a big area, and it suited him.

He didn't stop immediately but kept swimming slowly around. Finally, he settled in the middle, not the deepest or the shallowest. The current was still strong here, and he had to keep moving to remain in one place.

After a day or two, it stopped raining, and the river started to drop and clear up. He felt a little confined. It had been a long time since he had been in a river, but he did remember.

As the water cleared, he slowly moved around the hole. He saw a lot of animals and plants that brought back memories. He saw fish, many fish of all sizes, some just the right size to grab and eat, but he didn't.

There were other mature salmon in the water with him—not as big as him, of course, but some were good sized.

All the fish moved away when he got near, which was expected.

He had been in the river for about a week and was feeling his body maturing—or, in other words, getting ready to spawn. He had started to get the freshwater slime on his body, and he wasn't as silver in color as he had been. He had a rather dullish look.

The river had dropped so much that now, when he swam up to the upper end of the hole and on up into the riffles above it, his back would be out of the water. So he would turn around again and go back to the deep water.

Some of the smaller salmon staying around him would leave during the nights. Their smaller size allowed them to get over the riffles.

It didn't bother him that he couldn't leave. He wasn't ready to spawn anyway. He did smell the waters of the tributary, Moon Creek, his destination. It was faint, so he knew he had a distance to travel.

CHAPTER 28

Every so often, the big Chinook would give in to his natural instincts and chase a small trout or salmon around in the deep part of the river where he was holding. Sometimes he would grab and kill the little fish. He couldn't swallow it, although he did try once or twice. He did get one down, but then he regurgitated it back up.

This didn't bother him. He wasn't hungry anyway.

One day as he was lying in the deep part, facing upriver, there was a splash in the riffles, and then some salmon eggs with a crawly thing attached came floating by just above him. This wasn't an unusual thing to see, because he had seen a number them over the last few days as the water cleared.

Also, over the last few days he had been bothered by large shadows floating down from above him on the surface. He wasn't frightened, if that is the right word. He had seen similar shadows on the surface in the ocean.

But he was confined here and couldn't leave like he could in the ocean, and that fussed him up a little.

Earlier that day he had watched as one of his smaller brethren thrashed around in the river and eventually left. It was beyond his understanding, but it made him nervous.

When one of the crawly things—sand shrimp—came floating down the river right in front of him, he couldn't resist and grabbed it. He never even thought about it. It was there, and he took it, as he had so many in the past.

He didn't try to swallow it. He was just holding it in his mouth and squishing it when suddenly it bit him just behind his nose in the upper part of his mouth. He didn't move for a little while, and then he shook his head back and forth, trying to get rid of it because it was still giving him pain.

Finally, he started swimming around the deep part of the river and rubbed his nose in the mud and gravel, trying to dislodge it, to no avail.

What bothered him the most was that it was pulling him to the side, and he had to exert energy to keep upright and head a little in the opposite direction to compensate.

One time, he decided that the pain and irritation were not going away where he was, so he might as well leave. He headed upriver, over the riffles, and that didn't work out at all. He got to the point where he was halfway out of the water and was grounding out on the bottom with his stomach. Thrashing water, he turned around and went back. He felt the strain on his body with that maneuver, and it tired him a little. So he decided to lie in the deep part and rest, shaking his head now and then.

CHAPTER 29

Cork left Hebo and went directly to the Three Rivers parking lot on the Nestucca River. That was where a small river called Three Rivers ran into the big river.

It was quite popular with the sport fishermen. Not only was it a drift-boat launching area, but it was a good place to fish due the fact that the only state-owned fish hatchery in the Nestucca River area was up Three Rivers, and all the fish that came up the river must pass through it.

There was a large parking lot for the fishermen, maintained by Tillamook County, located up a short distance from the river, and that was where Johnathon had parked his vehicle. Cork came speeding in, slammed on his brakes, and parked.

Johnathon was about one quarter of a mile downriver, on private property. To get there, you had to cross a fence and put a couple of dollars in a can for the property owner.

Cork stopped at the fence, grabbed his billfold to get the two dollars, and found a five and a twenty.

Quietly saying a few choice words, he stuck the five-dollar bill in the can and took off running.

The trail followed the river for a short distance and then angled across a little open area before getting to the fishing hole where Johnathon was.

Cork, running on the trail along the river, tripped on a limb, fell on his butt, and slid a short distance down a gravel bank, ending up at the edge of the river. Muttering to himself, he sat there a few seconds wondering what the hell else was going to happen to him before he got to Johnathon.

He climbed back up the bank and took off again.

Coming out into the open space, Cork couldn't see Johnathon where he had left him. He stopped running, and, while walking, called out his name. But Johnathon didn't answer.

When he walked around a bunch of blackberry bushes where he could see better, there was Johnathon, sitting in the water near the bank, holding his fishing pole up in the air.

As Cork climbed down the bank, he yelled, "What are you doing in the water?" But Johnathon didn't answer, and Cork continued walking toward him, asking, "Are you OK?"

Johnathon didn't answer him, and Cork, now very apprehensive, squatted down and put his hand on Johnathon's left shoulder as he looked into his face.

He knew immediately that Johnathon was in shock. His skin was pale, his eyes were dilated, there was saliva on his chin, and his mouth was hanging slightly open.

Cork tried to take the pole out of his hands, but they were clamped on to it so tight that he couldn't budge it.

He said "Johnathon, let go of pole and get out of the water."

Johnathon didn't move, bat an eye, or show any recognition.

The pole was slightly bent but not moving. Cork couldn't tell if the fish was still on the line, but he doubted it. He figured if it was, it probably looked as bad as his friend.

Now Cork was trying to pry Johnathon's fingers off the pole, but it just wasn't working. They wouldn't move, and he was afraid that he might break one.

Finally, with the pole in his left hand, just above Johnathon's, he bent down and yelled into his face to let go of the pole. Johnathon just looked straight ahead and didn't move.

Cork swung around with his right hand and slapped him on the right cheek. But he didn't move, so Cork really came around the next time and walloped him good, slightly knocking his head sideways.

That did it. Johnathon looked up at Cork and said, "What the hell did you do that for?"

Cork laughed out loud and said, "Let go of the damned pole, John."

He loosened his grip so Cork could jerk it out of his hands and throw it over to the side, into the water.

Johnathon said, "Damn you, Cork. Get that pole."

Cork said, "No, not until I get you out of the water and moving. And besides, that fish isn't on your line anymore. It's probably long gone."

He then grabbed Johnathon by the back of his coat and dragged him up onto the bank.

Grabbing Johnathon's left arm and throwing it over his shoulder, Cork tried to stand him up, but it wasn't working. He told Johnathon, "Damn it, John, you got to help me here. You weigh a ton, and I'm not Superman. We must get you up and walking."

Johnathon was rummy and couldn't think straight. He told Cork his legs were kind of numb and felt like rubber. He was having trouble standing, let alone walking.

Cork said that it was no wonder and then asked him, "How long have you been sitting in the water?"

Johnathon had to think for a second and then said he really didn't know. He had to think on it.

He added that he had been backing up with the fish coming at him when he slipped and fell. The fish went back out into the hole, and he had stayed there because he felt too tired to get up.

Johnathon, looking around, asked, "Where is my fishing pole?"

Cork said, "Over there in the water." He pointed back to where Johnathon had been sitting in the water.

Johnathon stopped and said, "Good grief. Go get it; that fish is still on the line."

Corked looked back at where the pole was and said, "There is no fish on that line anymore, John."

"The hell there isn't," Johnathon said rather loudly. "Damn it, Cork. You said that before. You were wrong then, and you are wrong now. Go get that pole!" Then, in a little calmer voice, he said, "I'm all right. I'll just stand here. I'm getting warmer now."

Cork started to let go, and Johnathon about fell. Cork held on to him, looking him right in face, and said, "You don't have brain one, damn it. That darned fish almost killed you, and you still won't give up."

He then led Johnathon up toward the steep part of the bank, where there was the large end of a drift log, and helped him sit down on it. He asked Johnathon if he wanted him to build a fire to warm up. Johnathon replied that he was already warm, and "please" would he go and get his pole.

Cork shook his head, turned around, and stomped back down to the river's edge, muttering, "Jesus Christ."

He waded out into the water thinking how glad he was that he hadn't taken his rubber boots off earlier at home, like he usually did.

He reached down into the water, which was only about a foot deep, picked up the pole, and kind of shook it as the water ran off and out of the reel. He was surprised that the line still had tension on it as he lifted it.

CHAPTER 30

Cork turned back toward the shore and Johnathon and said "See?" He was going to add "There's no fish on it," but just as he got the "see" out of his mouth, he thought he felt a slight movement on the pole and turned back toward the river.

At first he couldn't feel any more of what he had thought was a movement. He clamped his thumb down on the reel spool and started backing up out of the water and putting more pressure on the pole.

He put a lot of pressure on the pole. He had decided that he was going to make something happen—either break the pole or line or move whatever was on the other end of it.

To his surprise, it gradually started to come toward him. He was dragging something in very slowly but still could not feel any movement. It felt like he was pulling in a waterlogged piece of wood or limb.

He kept pulling very slowly, and when he got up the bank, he reeled down to the water's edge again and then repeated the process.

He had done that three or four times when he thought he could almost see, down in the deep greenish-brown water, what he was pulling out.

He just couldn't make it out. It looked like a piece of a log or something similar.

And then Cork had what was just about the biggest shock of his life. He had gotten it a little closer and could see it clearly. It was undoubtedly the biggest salmon that he had ever seen in his life. It was absolutely huge. He stopped pulling and said out loud, very loud, "Oh my God, John."

Suddenly, Johnathon was standing right beside Cork, and he said, "Big fish, huh?"

Cork asked Johnathon if he had seen the fish before Cork had gotten back, and he said yes. He had seen it three or four times and had decided there was no way that he could land that fish by himself. That was the reason Cork had found him still sitting in the water, just holding the pole.

Now the fish was in the shallows. He was still in about three feet of water and was on the bottom, but his dorsal fin and the top of his tail were out of the water.

He hadn't come in headfirst or even sideways. He had come in angled at about forty-five degrees away from the beach. When he got close, Cork pulled his head around so the fish was parallel. His tail was slowly moving back and forth, but he didn't seem to mind being pulled by the fishing pole until he kind of grounded out on the bottom.

And then he just turned his head back toward the hole, and, of course, Cork could do nothing to stop it.

The fish went back down in the deepest part of the hole and stopped.

Corked turned and looked at Johnathon and said, "I haven't seen anything like that. That fish is longer than we are tall, and I'm six feet. That salmon must be eighty or so inches long. John, that fish must be a world record and weigh between one hundred fifty and two hundred pounds."

Both men just stood there and looked out into the river without saying a word for a good minute.

Finally, Cork said, "Maybe we should go get some help. A boat wouldn't be any good. There's no way anybody could lift that fish into a boat. Heck, it would sink the boat just trying to do it."

They both stood silent for a little longer, and then Johnathon asked, "Do you still carry a pistol under your seat in the pickup?"

Cork said, "Matter of fact, I do, but I'm not using it on a fish." And then he turned to face Johnathon. "There is no way that I'm going to shoot that salmon, John. Besides, I think it's still illegal."

Still thinking, Johnathon said, "Well, I have a big gaff at home, but that's illegal too. Christ, Cork, if we stuck a gaff in that fish, he would probably pull us both into the river or hurt us, anyway."

"You know, we might get hurt trying to land that fish any way you look at it," Cork quietly added.

He had no more than said that when the fish started to slowly move upstream. Cork didn't try to turn him—that would have been impossible—but he did keep a tight line so there was still pressure pulling back on the fish's movements.

Cork asked Johnathon, "Did he try to leave while I was gone?"

"He didn't try to go downstream, back to the ocean, but he did try to go upstream three times. The water is just too shallow. He couldn't make it, but he sure raised havoc trying. He threw water everywhere. In fact," Johnathon said, "one time I thought he was going to end up out into the farmers field because when he turned back, that was where he was headed."

Johnathon went on to say that if it had been a smaller fish, he could have possibly turned it into the shallows and beached it. But not anything that big.

The fish kept slowly moving, and Cork and Johnathon walked up the gravel beach alongside it but slightly downstream.

When the fish started into the very shallow area, it hesitated, apparently trying to decide what to do—try again or go back?

Finally, it took off, throwing water everywhere. It traveled about twenty-five yards and then had to stop. The water was only around twelve inches deep, and the fish was grounded out. It didn't have enough water to push itself forward anymore.

It didn't have enough water to stay upright, and it lay over on its side and drifted downstream a couple of times. Then, after two or three tries, it gave up, and, after drifting farther downstream on its side, it righted itself and headed back down.

After the fish got back to the deep water and turned around again, Cork looked over at Johnathon and told him that if it had gotten another twenty feet up that riffle, it would have made it, and they would never have stopped it. Johnathon agreed.

Cork brought up the idea of him going up to the Hebo Sporting Goods store and getting some help or just calling some of their friends to bring some ropes.

Johnathon looked at Cork and said, "What the hell are you going to do with ropes? That isn't any cow out there, for God's sake. Anybody who gets a rope around that fish's tail will end up in the river, and you know it."

Cork didn't say anything for a couple of seconds, and then he said, "Well, you're probably right. But we got to think of something, or one of us is probably going to get hurt." And then he added, "There's no way we're going to get a landing net over it. They just don't make them that big. At least I've never seen one."

Meanwhile, Cork started pulling hard on the fish again. Just like the last time, it started coming slowly toward the gravel beach that Cork and Johnathon were standing on.

Johnathon said, "The fish is tired. There's no doubt about that."

Cork said, "Well, it ought to be. How many hours has it been? Four or five at least, and it looked like he almost won by the way you looked when I got back here a while ago. By the way, didn't any boats or other bank anglers come by while I was gone?"

Johnathon acknowledged that two boats had come downriver, but no bank anglers. He told the people in the boats that he was hung up on the bottom because the fish wasn't moving, and it looked that way. Neither boat stayed around very long.

Cork said, "I absolutely cannot understand how that hook stayed in the fish so long without pulling out or just falling out. It had to have worked itself loose by now. And another thing. That fish must have huge sharp teeth because of his size. The line must have crossed them at least once. How come the line didn't break?"

Johnathon had to admit he was a little perplexed about that too. He thought maybe the hook was so far forward in the upper jaw that the line never crossed the teeth and that it must be embedded in bone so that it couldn't move.

Whatever the reason, luck must have a lot to do with it.

CHAPTER 31

The men finally got the fish in sight again, still angled away from them and swimming slowly but nevertheless coming into the shallow area around the beach where Cork and Johnathon were standing.

When it was only about fifteen feet from them but still totally underwater, Johnathon told Cork to quit pulling, that he just wanted to look at the fish. He knew the fish could come off the line at any time, and he wanted to have a good look at it before it did. Cork agreed because he felt the same way and said so.

The fish was huge and had a ferocious look about his eyes and face, probably just because of his size. But it was noticeable, and Cork mentioned it.

Johnathon took his eyes off the fish and looked at Cork, saying that he had never heard him say a fish looked mean before. Cork replied, probably because he had never said it or thought it before, but that fish looked "damned mean."

They both stood still and looked at the fish for a couple of minutes. It was just lying there with its tail slowly going back and forth, not trying to get away. But Cork still had a lot of pressure on the pole.

The fish's head had pulled around, and it was lying parallel with the beach. It inched closer until the dorsal fin started to touch the surface. It was still in, probably, four feet of water.

Cork said that he hated to keep repeating himself about the fish being huge. "My God, how much do you think it weighs?"

Johnathon just shook his head and had no idea but said, "Cork, you and I have weighed a lot of fish, deer, elk, and other big critters in our day. I don't know about you, but I have never weighed anything like that."

Cork told Johnathon about weighing a halibut in Alaska that weighed two hundred and some pounds. That was the biggest fish. He turned slightly, looking at Johnathon, and said, "John, this fish looks almost as big. It's at least a hundred and fifty.

"If we land it, it will be the biggest salmon on record. There's no doubt about that, and you're going to be famous. Your face is going to be in every paper and on every TV in the county. You're probably going to have to tell the story of how you caught it, a thousand times."

Cork thought for a minute, and then he smiled and started chuckling. "Hell, the president will probably want your autograph and to hear the story." He burst out laughing.

Johnathon wasn't laughing. He appeared in deep thought when he quietly said, "You asshole. You just remember you're here too. Your name will be right beside mine."

Cork quit laughing—or smiling, for that matter. He said, "I would appreciate not being involved, if you don't mind. Of course, since I'm probably the best and only good friend you got, I'm sure you will keep my name out of the spotlight, huh?"

Johnathon didn't say a word, but Cork's little speech made him smile a little bit.

He was looking at the head of the fish now, about ten feet away. He said, "Cork, look at its eyes. It's looking at us. Just watch when I move. His eyes, at least the one on this side, will follow me."

It was easy to see the fish's eyes, since the water was reasonably clear and the fish was so close. Cork did as Johnathon said.

It did look as if the fish was watching Johnathon, but he thought it must be an illusion. He had never heard of such a thing.

Cork asked, "John, are we going to try to get it on the beach now or just stand here and look at it?"

They both agreed that to beach the fish, they would have to get it on its side and slide it up. For them to do that, it would have to be completely exhausted. And even then, they would have to lay the pole down and manhandle it. One of them would have to pull it by the gills and the other push it by the tail.

It would not be easy, and it could be dangerous if the fish got a burst of energy and started thrashing, which had happened to both men with smaller fish.

CHAPTER 32

Cork held the pole but slacked off a little while Johnathon slowly waded out to the fish. He reached down and touched it about two feet in front of the tail, and then all hell busted loose.

Water flew everywhere; Johnathon went flying back, full length, into the water; and Cork, who had tightened up the drag on the reel a little, trying to hold the fish in place, was jerked straight forward onto his knees and into the water before he could loosen it back up.

Of course, the fish went back into the deep water, and the two men just sat in the water where they had ended up. At first it was not a happy situation, and they looked at each other, with water running off and frowns on their faces.

Cork asked, "John, you all right?"

"I think so. Just good and wet. I think I went airborne for a couple of feet."

They were both still sitting in the water, and Cork said, "I don't think you should have touched it yet."

Johnathon replied, "Oh, really?" And they both started laughing.

Cork, still in the water holding the pole, added, "You know, that fish may end up bagging us instead of us getting him. Maybe we should get him in close again and cut the line."

This time Johnathon was not so set against the idea, because he had to think about it for a couple of seconds. And then he replied, "Cork, I have fought that fish for the good part of the day. I'm tired, I'm almost totally soaked, and I hurt damned near all over. I even thought I had a heart attack one time. I'm going to think on that idea, but I'm not ready to quit just yet."

Neither one of them was laughing anymore, and as they were standing up out of the water, Cork said, "I'll stay with you, bud. It's your decision. Somehow, we'll get that fish in here. Just remember what I told you. When I go, don't let anyone put me in the ground. Spread my ashes down this river and in the mountains."

Johnathon had been walking out of the water up to the bank, and he stopped, turned to Cork, and said, "You ass." And they both started laughing again.

The fish hadn't moved since going back into the deep part of the hole, and Cork didn't try to pull him back out just yet. He had to take time to rest and think.

He wasn't sure that fish, as big as it was, would ever get tired or docile enough for John and him to get it out of the river and up on the bank. If they could just get his head out of the water, he could hit him with a rock or piece of driftwood. That might do it, but he didn't even know if that would work.

One thing for sure: before they could manhandle him out of the river, they were going to have to kill or stun him somehow. If they tried it any other way, one of them, or maybe both, was liable to get a busted leg or worse.

For John to get slapped with the tail just proved that the fish was so big that it wasn't using up all its energy. It was keeping some in reserve, probably by instinct, to survive and still get up the river to spawn.

Anyone could tell that the fish hadn't been out of the ocean for very long, so it hadn't used up much protein from lack of food intake, and it had plenty in reserve.

While Cork was still standing at the water's edge with the pole in his hand, Johnathon walked up from the beach and lay down in the grass where the sun was still shining, to dry off. Or at least try.

Cork yelled over at him and asked if he had eaten anything. Johnathon said no, he hadn't brought a lunch because he hadn't planned on staying that long.

Cork said, "That figures." While holding the pole with his left hand, he took two energy bars out of his coat pocket with his right and threw them to him. He always carried the two bars, and he hadn't eaten them that day because he had made a lunch and eaten it earlier.

Johnathon, who was really famished, grabbed the bars and ate them rapidly and then took his bottle of water out of his coat pocket and drank what was left.

He said, "Thanks, Cork. I really needed that." And then he lay back down in the grass.

The fish started to move. Not fast at first, just slowly circling the deep water. It didn't appear that he was trying to leave. And then he started to go faster and faster until he had muddied up the deep hole so bad that visibility was down to zero and dead leaves and sticks were all over surface. He had done this before, but not to this extreme.

Johnathon got up from the grass and came over to stand by Cork and watch.

After a couple of minutes, he said, "I wonder what it's up to. I thought it was getting tired, but it looks like I was wrong."

It turned just in front of the two men toward the opposite shore and sped up. When it reached the approximate middle of the river, without warning and to the men's total surprise, it came straight up and completely out of the water. Its mouth was open, and it was thrashing back and forth. It was huge and totally pissed off.

Corked yelled, "Holy shit. Look at that!"

And Johnathon muttered, "Oh, my God" at the same time.

When it fell back, it hit the water on its side, and water flew everywhere because it didn't quit thrashing until it was deep underneath.

Both men, who had been standing at the water's edge, had water lap up over the toes of their boots from the turbulence.

Cork looked at Johnathon and said, "Now, John, tell me that salmon didn't look really, really mad to you."

"Yeah, it did," said Johnathon. "And did you hear that growl? It sounded like a lion to me. How about you?"

Johnathon was grinning when Cork gave him a questioning look and then called him a choice name.

The fish started to settle down again, and, after slowly making another circle, it stopped in its usual spot, the deepest part of the hole.

Cork said that he had almost lost the pole when the fish came out and threw his head to the side. It was a wonder the pole didn't bust, because the drag was still set tight. It didn't help, and Cork held up his right thumb to show Johnathon the large blister starting to show.

Johnathon held up his hand with his thumb in the air, saying, "Yeah, I have one of those too."

CHAPTER 33

Johnathon informed Cork that the energy bars really helped, and he felt a lot better. He thought he could handle the pole again. Cork looked like he needed a break, which he did, and he gave the pole to Johnathon.

Cork started rubbing his hands and shoulders with a grimace on his face. He said, "You know, I said this before, and I'll say it again. We are too damned old to be doing this crap! We should cut the line and let that fish go. Hell, John, it's going to be dark in a couple of hours, and I don't think our wives are going to take kindly to us spending the night on the river like we did twenty years ago."

He went on. "And besides, you and I both have all the salmon we need to eat in our freezers. We don't need this fish. It would probably fill up an entire freezer.

Can you imagine trying to find a frying pan—or even a barbeque, for that matter—big enough to fry a steak off that fish? Impossible. Totally impossible."

They both laughed.

Johnathon stopped smiling and said, "Cork, you know as well as I do why I want to catch that fish. It's big, the biggest salmon that I have ever seen or heard about, and probably the biggest salmon that *anyone* has ever seen or heard about. Not that I need any bragging material. It's just for myself—to know that *I* did it. And I know you know what I'm talking about, so don't stand there and read me the riot act.

"Besides, what the hell else have you got to do anyway? And if we get hurt doing this...well, I know you've been hurt bad before. I'm sure we'll live through it. Anyway, I think and hope we live through it."

He sheepishly looked over at Cork and grinned again.

Cork was not smiling. He opened his mouth to say something, closed it, and then said, "When you are laying in the hospital with a broken leg or something, I'm going to remember you said that, John."

He was starting to walk off the beach and up the bank when Johnathon said, "Where are you going?"

Cork told him that he was going to look for a large limb on a willow that had a good fork on it. He went on to say that the only thing he could think of was to try to get the fork under the fish's gill plate, and then one of them could try to pull or at least head the fish up the beach and out of the water, if and when they got it that far. He added that the other person could push from behind.

Cork had stopped climbing up the bank when talking to Johnathon, and when he had finished, there were a few moments of silence. Then Johnathon asked, "Are you telling me you are going to try to pull a fish that size out of the water on a willow limb?" He wasn't smiling.

"If you have any better ideas, John, I would like to hear them now." Cork continued up the bank.

He came back in about five minutes towing a branch that was probably eight feet long and four inches around at the base, where there was a large fork protruding that he had sharpened.

Johnathon still had the pole in his hands and watched as Cork climbed down the bank with the large limb and laid it down on the beach.

He told Johnathon that the only bad thing about sticking that fork in the fish's gill plate was that it would undoubtedly injure the gills, and if the fish got away after that, he would start bleeding and die before getting upriver.

Not only did Johnathon agree, but he said, "I don't want to use that."

Cork said that they wouldn't unless they had to.

Although the fish had put on quite an exhibition earlier, it was getting tired. It was still lying close to the bottom in the deep area when Johnathon started to put pressure on the pole in an attempt to pull it toward the beach again.

It was working, as before. The fish was gradually being pulled sideways but slightly angled away.

It was getting closer when Cork said, "John, now don't do anything stupid."

Johnathon looked over at him, and Cork said, "If that fish gets on top of you, I'm going to cut the line. I mean it."

As Johnathon got the fish close enough to touch, Cork did just that.

He waded out about six feet, to where he could reach down and forward and touch the fish's dorsal fin.

The fish had been slowly moving his tail back and forth while being pulled by Johnathon, but when Cork touched it with his finger, it stopped.

Cork took his hand away, and the tail started to move again. Cork reached back and touched the fish but behind the dorsal fin, and he used his whole hand this time.

The fish quit moving its tail again, so Cork left his hand on the fish.

It didn't do anything, so Cork started moving his hand back and forth slowly, like he was petting it. It still didn't move away, but it did slowly swing its head around, so it looked like it was looking at the men with its right eye.

Cork looked back at Johnathon and said, "Good God, I feel like I am taming a monster." He grinned.

Johnathon, who had quit pulling so hard on the pole, said, "Do you have any idea what to do next?"

Cork said, "Absolutely not."

CHAPTER 34

The men didn't know how to proceed because they had never handled a fish that big that was still very much alive and still in the water.

It seemed to be tired, but it had appeared this way before. And then it jumped clear out of the water after almost hurting them both.

They had seen what the fish was capable of, thrashing around on and below the surface. The speed it could obtain in a very short time was unbelievable for anything of such size.

There was no doubt in either man's mind that if they did manage to get the fish on the beach, in or out of the shallow water, and it went crazy, like some fish do, one if not both of them was going to get hurt.

The men were older and slower than they used to be, and they knew they couldn't react fast enough to get out of the way.

After the fish calmed down, Johnathon asked, "Cork, do you see any blood coming from the gills?"

Cork looked at the front of the fish and said, "No, but I can't see the other side." And then he added, "If there is, it can't be much."

The fish still wasn't moving his tail, so Johnathon decided to try to pull its head around toward the beach.

He knew better than to touch the line, so he clamped his thumb down on the reel's spool so it wouldn't give out line under pressure, and he started to back up.

The fish's body started to turn toward Johnathon and away from the river. He kept a steady pressure on the line and pole. Its mouth was opening and closing in conjunction with the gill plates moving back and forth with the flow of water.

For all intents and purposes, the fish looked tired, but Johnathon and Cork both knew that all hell could break loose at any second, and the result could be catastrophic.

Finally, its belly touched the gravel bottom, and it immediately stopped. Johnathon quit pulling on the line, and gradually the fish started to move backward, away from the beach.

Cork said, "John, keep pulling."

Johnathon replied, "I am, damn it. Can't you see?"

The fish kept gradually moving back, and Cork, still with his hand on its back and an astonished look on his face, said, "Good grief, this thing is swimming backward. I have never seen a fish swim backward before, have you?"

"Hell no," Johnathon said. "I didn't think it was possible, but look at its pectoral fins. They're pushing forward, toward me. I can't see the lower ones, but I bet they're doing the same."

"I don't think we should try to hold it, do you?"

"No, John. Just keep pressure on the pole, like you're doing. We'll just let it go back out in the river and then do this all over again." Cork took his hand off the fish as it moved away.

The fish moved back into deeper water, turned, headed back to the middle where it usually lay, and stopped.

Cork said, "I don't believe this is happening."

Johnathon said, "It's like tying a fishing line to the bumper of a car and trying to lead the car around with a fish pole."

Then, with a grin on his face, he turned slightly around toward Cork.

Cork was looking John right in the face and asked, "How in hell do you know that? Have you tried it or something?"

There was a moment of silence as they looked at each other, and then they both burst out laughing, probably more as a release from the stress and tension than anything else.

Cork finally said, "I'm going to remember you said that. I'm going to tell everyone we know how Johnathon Pane practices fighting and landing big fish at home. I bet you even have a big piece of cardboard painted like a fish's tail that you tie onto the rear bumper, huh?"

Johnathon asked, "Have I ever told you that you were an ass?"

Cork said, "Many times, my friend. Many times."

Of course, all of this just made them laugh harder.

CHAPTER 35

The men pulled the fish to the beach three times, and every time, it backed out again, turned around, and went back to the deepest spot in the hole.

The men were exhausted, cold, and hungry. They figured the fish had to be just about done in, but, of course, they had told themselves that hours ago.

Cork had taken over the pole a while back because Johnathon's left arm had cramped up again. As Johnathon stood there and rubbed his arm, he said, "You know, that fish is so heavy, it might just die out there in the river, and we couldn't pull it off the bottom."

It was quiet for a couple seconds, and then Cork said, "Actually, I would more apt to think we both might die out here on the beach before that fish does. I don't know if you've noticed, but it's starting to get dark."

"Oh, good," Johnathon said. "Lord, I thought that I was getting so tired that my eyelids were closing." Cork immediately turned around and looked, and Johnathon said, "I'm kidding, for gosh sakes. I'm fine."

Cork was grumbling to himself as he started to put pressure on the pole, to pull the fish in to the beach again.

This time, Cork noticed the fish was being pulled straight toward the beach, not angled away as before. It wasn't coming easy, but it wasn't struggling to get back to the deep water either.

As it was coming up into the shallower water, it started to lie over on its side when it touched the bottom with its stomach. The fish was finally giving up, and the men knew it. It was time. Even a fish that size has only so much; the battle was over.

Cork handed the pole to Johnathon, and they maneuvered the fish up to the beach, not totally out of the water but close. Its fins were still moving, and the gills were opening and closing in conjunction with its mouth.

When the fish came over on its side, the belly was directly in front of Cork. His eyes got big, and he said rather loudly, "Oh, shit."

Johnathon asked, "What? What's wrong?"

Cork said, "We thought this was a male. It's a female. Look at the size of her pooper. It must be the size of a half dollar, and now that I can see her profile, there's no doubt. This fish is a *female*."

He was holding the fish in front of the tail with both hands. Although she was on her side, her tail was still moving a little, and his arms were moving up and down. He looked over at Johnathon, who was quiet and appeared in deep thought.

Johnathon slacked off the pole. He reached down with his left hand and removed the hook, which was in the upper part of the fish's mouth, just behind the nose.

He looked over at Cork, shook his head, stood up, walked up to the beach, and laid his pole down. He then turned around, walked back to Cork and the fish, and said, "Well, that cinches it. Let's let it go."

"Are you sure, John? You've been through a lot with it, and it's definitely a world record. That's for sure. I mean, I just want you to realize what you're giving up. And besides, I'm not real sure she'll make it. You fought her a long time."

They gradually uprighted the fish and turned her around, which was not an easy task. Both men were in over their boots and up to their waists in the water. When they got her headed facing the middle of the river, they started moving back and forth, trying to get water passing through her mouth and gills.

The process was difficult. It was a struggle just to keep her from lying over on her side. She was so heavy and slippery, and the men were so tired and cold.

Cork was worried about Johnathon and kept asking him how he was doing. Finally, getting tired of it, Johnathon told him to be quiet and if he passed out, to just let him float down the river.

Cork informed him that he was being the asshole now. They both were smiling but too tired to laugh.

They worked with the fish for a good half hour, but she just wouldn't stay upright. If they let go of her, she gradually would lie over on her side.

Cork told Johnathon that they might have to put her out of her misery and try to get her home. He didn't know how much longer they could stand being in the water without getting hyperthermia, and if they both lost control, they would be in a lot of trouble. The only reason they hadn't succumbed already was the fact that they were constantly moving.

Johnathon wanted to try a little while longer. But he noticed that his hands were starting to shake, and he knew that wasn't a good sign. He didn't tell Cork, though. He knew what he would say.

It was getting dark when Johnathon said, "Hey, Cork, do you have a measuring tape in your coat? You usually do."

Cork dug around in his pocket with one hand while he tried to hold the fish with the other. He smiled and held up the measuring tape.

He handed the end of the tape to Johnathon, who held it at the fish's nose as Cork took the tape to the end of her tail. He yelled at Johnathon, "OK, I got it. Let go." And he did. Cork quickly put the tape back in his pocket and grabbed the fish again as it started to lie over.

Johnathon asked, "Well, what the hell was it? Or were you planning on not telling me?"

Cork looked over at him and said, "No, no. I was just thinking that there was no way we could tell anyone about this. No one would believe us, ever."

He smiled and added, "Oh, it measured eighty and one-half inches long. What do you think about those bacons, John?"

Johnathon, smiling, said, "Wow. You're right. No one will believe it, so we might as well keep it to ourselves, huh? And, by the way, as I have told you before, that is the stupidest expression that I think I've ever heard."

They both started laughing, more from being totally exhausted than anything else.

The fish started to stay upright longer after they took their hands away, and finally it didn't lie over at all. She looked normal. All her fins were moving slowly, but they were moving.

The men were still moving her back and forth in the water but were coming to a point where they could not do it any longer.

They finally stopped and hung their arms down, totally done in.

The fish just lay there suspended, not touching bottom and no part of her body out of the water.

After about five minutes, Johnathon asked, "Do you think we should push her out?"

Cork didn't have an answer. "Hell, I don't know. I don't know, John. I think I'm too tired to do even that."

The fish started to move, slowly at first and then inching her way off the shallow bar and into the deep water at the edge of the current. And there she stayed, acquiring more oxygen from the current.

The men couldn't see her anymore, of course—not only because of the deeper water, but because it was almost totally dark now.

CHAPTER 36

Johnathon fell to his knees, and Cork splashed over and grabbed him. He dragged him up to the beach and pulled him out of the water.

Asked if he thought he could walk, he gave no answer. He just mumbled.

Cork thought, Full-blown hyperthermia or worse. He knew he couldn't get Johnathon up to the parking lot, and with both cell phones not working, it would probably take him too long to get help because he could hardly walk either. He started picking up all the dry wood that he could find.

He had some dry paper in the form of gas receipts in his billfold, which he had put in his breast pocket when he started to get wet. He got them out and grabbed the book matches that he kept in his billfold for emergencies and tried to start a fire on the beach about six feet from Johnathon.

Cork was cold and wet and going into hyperthermia also. He was shaking so hard that he was having trouble striking a match. And then, when he finally succeeded, the twigs wouldn't catch and the paper burned out.

He got his last receipt and his twenty dollar bill out and tried again. As he hurried as fast as he could with tears running down his cheeks because he thought he might be too late, the twigs caught, and cork started pilling on the branches.

He had a good-sized fire going, including a lot of smoke since a lot of the wood was wet, and he started dragging Johnathon up to it. Johnathon did not appear to be conscious, but he was mumbling, which Cork took as a good sign.

He started taking his wet clothes off. Starting with his coat, he wrung as much water out of each article as he could, and then he laid them out on the rocks around the fire.

Cork's own coat was not completely wet, so he replaced Johnathon's with his own.

He found a small drift log with some broken limbs still attached and pulled it up to the fire. He took his own and Johnathon's socks off and hung them on the limbs until they started steaming, and then he rolled them up and put them under his armpits and on his stomach, trying to get his core temperature up. When the socks cooled off, he hung them up near the fire again. After he had done this three times, the socks were dry.

Meanwhile, Cork kept rubbing Johnathon's arms and shoulders and talking to him. Any clothes that appeared warm and dry, including his own, he threw on him.

It didn't take long before Cork, working around the hot fire, had recovered and not only started to dry out himself but was sweating.

With his back turned to Johnathon as he attended the fire, he heard him say, "Damn, if you aren't the ugliest nurse that I've ever had."

Turning around and laughing, Cork said, "About time you came around. I was beginning to wonder if you were going to leave me with this mess you caused, you old fool." This got them both laughing, probably from relief more than anything else.

Johnathon, trying to move and look around, added, "Good grief, most of your clothes are on me. Aren't you cold?"

Cork said, "Not one bit. In fact, I feel like I'm roasting."

Johnathon reached under the coat that was over him, which was Cork's, and pulled out a large white sock. He held it up in the firelight and looked at it, saying, "Is this yours? Because it sure isn't mine."

Cork, still grinning, said, "Matter of fact, it is. It's wool, and yours are cotton. Wool retains the heat more than cotton. I've been heating them up and putting them around your stomach to warm you up. And apparently it worked, because you're still here. I think you got close to the line, bud. You scared the hell out of me."

Cork stood up. He heard a car horn up in the parking lot. He said, "John, you just stay where you are. I think someone has come looking for us. I had better go see."

Cork finished pulling his wet boots on—without socks, which is hard to do—and walked up and over the bank. He was about halfway there when he saw a couple of flashlights coming toward him. He yelled "Hello" and immediately got a reply. "Cork, is that you?" It was Linda.

"Yes," he yelled back. "Who's with you?"

"Lucy." And then, "What are you still doing down here this late anyway?"

When they got to him, Cork asked Linda if she had her cell phone with her, explaining that his was dead. That was the reason that he had not called.

She handed hers to him and asked why he wanted it, but he didn't reply. He was touching 911 and got an instant answer.

He explained that he needed an ambulance at the Three Rivers boat landing on the Nestucca river for the transport of a patient showing signs of hyperthermia and possible heart attack or stroke.

He gave the operator his name and answers to all her questions. When he turned back around to Lucy and Linda, they were gone. He could see their flashlights downriver just before they went out of sight over the bank.

Cork headed in the opposite direction, toward the parking lot, to wait for the ambulance, knowing Johnathon was in good hands. He would probably give Cork the dickens for leaving him with both of those females. They were probably giving him a nonstop scolding for being on the river so late and fussing over him like only those two could.

He had left Johnathon about half naked, getting warm by the fire, and he was not the type to show bare skin in front of any woman besides his wife. Thinking about it, Cork started to chuckle, imagining the scolding he was going to get from Johnathon when he recovered.

CHAPTER 37

It only took about five minutes for the ambulance to arrive. Cork figured it must have come from Cloverdale, which was only about three miles away.

He told the EMTs where Johnathon was and why he had called for them, suspecting a heart problem besides the hyperthermia.

There were three attendants in the ambulance, and after they were ready with their equipment and stretcher, Cork led them down the riverbank.

Cork could see the fire long before they got to the bend in the river. The girls must have been frightened and piled all the dry wood on the fire that they could find.

Linda came running up to Cork when he started down the riverbank. She asked, "Did you know John has a heart valve problem and has had it for several years?"

Cork stopped and stood there for a few seconds, thinking, and then said, "Hell no. He never told me anything about it. That explains a lot about how he's been acting, grabbing his chest and all."

Linda said, "He was asleep or unconscious when we got here, but he's awake now."

Cork looked over at Johnathon. The EMTs had arrived and surrounded him with their equipment, talking and doing their thing. Cork had all the confidence in the world in them. He had worked with them for many years while in law enforcement. They were a highly trained and efficient bunch of people, and he knew Johnathon was in good hands.

Lucy walked up to him and said, "Boy, that must have been a big salmon to fight that long. Too bad you guys lost it."

Cork asked, "Oh, John must have told you about it, huh?"

"Oh, yes, he told me how he fought that fish for almost six hours, and finally the hook just fell out. That it was the biggest salmon he had ever had on, and it probably weighed fifty or sixty pounds."

Cork almost opened his mouth and corrected her, but, after second thought, he kept it shut, figuring John had his reasons for telling Lucy that story. He was sure he would hear about it later.

Linda knew something was up. She knew Cork too well and saw by his expression that he was a little upset at what Lucy had said. So, after Lucy went back to the group, she asked Cork what had really happened.

Cork just shook his head and told her he would tell her later when they were by themselves, and then he walked over to one of the EMTs and asked if he could help.

They had Johnathon on the stretcher, and, of course, he was having a fit. He kept saying he could walk to the parking lot, and one of the EMTs was telling him that he wasn't walking anywhere right now and to just lie back and enjoy the ride.

Finally, one of them came over to Cork and said they were headed back and that they would be taking him to the Tillamook Hospital.

Lucy intended to go in the ambulance with Johnathon, so she got his keys to the pickup and gave them to Linda so she and Cork could ferry it to the hospital. She had ridden down to the parking lot with Linda, so there was not an extra car. Cork would pick his truck up on the way back from the hospital to drive it home.

They took off with Johnathon and the stretcher after just about accidentally dumping him off getting up the bank. A lot of yelling and cussing tool place, and they were off again.

Cork and Linda stayed to put out the fire and picked up some of the clothes that were left behind.

Cork said, "Boy, that John—he can be cantankerous sometimes."

Linda said, "And I suppose you can't. I think you both came out of the same mold." She was looking at Cork while picking up a coat. She was grinning.

Cork stopped spreading out the hot coals, turned to her, and with a smile said, "Come on, I'm not that bad, am I?"

They both started chuckling.

They cleaned up the beach and were just getting to the parking lot when Cork told Linda that he was going to leave his pickup and drive John's to the hospital. He wanted Linda to follow in her car. She decided that was as good a plan as any. That way, Lucy would have transportation if John had to stay.

CHAPTER 38

When they got to the hospital, Johnathon was still in emergency. He hadn't seen a doctor yet, and, of course, he was in a bad mood and making life miserable for everyone around him.

The head nurse, whose name was Sally, had already told him to shut up two or three times, and the last time she threatened to gag him with a towel. The threat was taken good-naturedly, but Cork got the impression that maybe she really meant it.

Johnathon had three major problems: hospitals in general, doctors of any kind, and anyone who stuck needles in him. Of course, just about everyone in the emergency section of the hospital fit in one of those categories.

Lucy approached Cork when they arrived and asked him to try to calm Johnathon down. He was getting rather embarrassing.

Cork walked up to him and, without saying a word, just stared.

Johnathon wasn't looking at him at first. And then, turning his head, he said, "What the hell are you looking at?"

Cork said, "Well, if you really want an answer to that, then I would probably say a fool, or at least someone who's trying to act like one."

Johnathon didn't like that. "Why did you call an ambulance? Now, get me out of here, damn it."

"No, I will not. You lay right there and let a doctor look at you, John. You've been through a lot today. You've been unconscious at least three times, and if you don't, I'm going to tell Lucy the truth and anybody else that will listen about what went on today with your fifty- or sixty-pound chinook."

Johnathon's eyes got big, and he was silent for a good fifteen seconds. And then he said, "Apparently, Lucy must have told you what I said." He looked all around the room to see who was within hearing distance.

"Why in heaven's name would you tell Lucy that?" Cork asked. "Are you ashamed to admit that you released the world's biggest salmon that's ever existed?"

"No, I'm not ashamed of it. It's just that those EMTs were listening, and I didn't what to be questioned about it and somebody to tell me how crazy I am."

Cork said, "Well, it was kind of a crazy thing to do; I have to admit that. What do you want me to tell Linda and anyone else who asks me about what happened today? Everyone we know is going to ask about you and how come you're in here. I'm not very good at lying, as you well know."

"Hell, Cork, nobody is going to believe us if we tell them what really happened, and you know it. Why don't we just say it was a great big fish and leave it at that?"

"OK, we won't tell anyone how huge it was except for Linda. I've never lied to Linda, and I'm not going to start, especially over a damned fish. And you had better tell Lucy the truth too, or you'll really be in for it if she finds out."

Johnathon was quiet for a few seconds, and then, calmly and in thought, he said, "She's already mad at me, which is not an unusual thing, as you well know."

Cork smiled but didn't add anything. He knew how Lucy could be.

About that time, a doctor and a couple of nurses came through the curtain divider. One was Sally, the department's head nurse. She looked at Cork and with a nod motioned him to leave, which he did immediately.

He went to the waiting room, where Lucy and Linda had been sitting since Cork had gone in to talk to Johnathon.

As he sat down, he noticed both women were looking at him with questioning looks in the eyes. He told them that the doctor was with John now, so it would probably be a little while before they had any news.

After a few minutes, Lucy told Cork that Johnathon had lied to her about what happened on the river, and she would like to know the truth. She added that she could always tell when he lied to her because he couldn't look her in the eye.

Corked laughed a little and said, "It wasn't much of a lie. John just didn't want you to know the size of the fish, and he released it instead of the fish getting off the hook by itself. He didn't want the EMTs to hear about it. He'll probably tell you the whole story when you get alone with him."

Lucy said, "I don't trust you either. You would lie for him in a minute, and don't think I don't know it. Was he with another woman or something?"

Cork about fell out of his chair, and Linda started laughing. He knew Lucy must be kidding. She wasn't smiling when she said it, but then she started to grin. Cork said, "Oh, Lord, no. I know that didn't happen for sure, and I think you do too. John would never do anything like that." Cork paused and then added, "Now, me." And he stopped, looking at Linda and laughing as she gave him a stern look and pointed her finger.

Turning back to Lucy, he continued. "Don't worry, Lucy. John has two loves in his life—you and Chinook salmon."

She said, "I know that. I was kidding. But between me and the salmon, I'm not real sure which one comes first."

They were all still laughing when Linda said, "It's terrible to think your competition is a fish, huh? I think I fall in the same category."

About five minutes later, after they had calmed down, the doctor came into the waiting room and told them that Johnathon had no doubt had a bad day, but since he was in pretty good shape, even with his heart condition, he was letting him go home. He had not had a heart attack, and he had lost consciousness probably due to exhaustion and dehydration. He advised Johnathon to get an appointment with his primary physician within the week as a follow-up.

He added, "Keeping an animal caged up overnight in the hospital would probably be more detrimental than good for everyone concerned."

They all had a good laugh over that, probably from relief more than his last comment.

CHAPTER 39

Lucy went behind the curtain to help Johnathon put his clothes on. His voice was loud and could be heard quite plainly throughout that part of the hospital.

His displeasure with the hospital gown and its airy backside was heard by most everyone within hearing distance.

When he pulled open the curtain and stomped out, he was totally pissed off and looked like he could chew nails. He walked up to Cork, thanked him for bringing his pickup to the hospital, and told him that he would call him the next day.

He then stomped out the door without saying another word. Lucy, throwing her arms in the air, followed after mouthing "Thank you" to Linda and Cork.

On the way to their vehicle, Linda asked Cork what really did happen down on the river. As they drove away, Cork started with the story of how Johnathon fought the biggest salmon in history to a standstill and damned near killed himself in doing it.

Linda said, "It's too bad you didn't have a camera to take a picture, or at least a measuring tape to measure it."

Cork, who was driving now, looked over at her and said, "I did have a measuring tape."

Linda said, "Well, did you use it or not?"

Cork, being tired and without a whole lot of patience, said a little loudly, "Linda, will you let me finish the story or not? Yes, I did use it, and the fish measured eighty and one-half inches from nose to tail."

Linda didn't say a word. She just sat there looking at Cork, and then she said, "You're kidding me, aren't you? No salmon could be that large, and you know it."

He didn't answer immediately. He acted like he was in deep thought about something else. He finally kind of shook his head and said, "Yes. I mean no, I'm not kidding. I measured it myself, and it measured eighty and one-half inches long. I would have liked to measure its girth, but to tell the truth, I was a little scared to try. I saw that fish knock John right off his feet. It's a wonder he didn't get hurt bad. Anyway, I figure it weighed in the neighborhood of two hundred pounds, give or take twenty or thirty."

Both Linda and Cork sat quiet for a couple of minutes, and then Linda asked Cork why Johnathon released it after fighting it for so long.

Cork said, "Honey, as you know, sometimes John can be a strange dude. But in this case, I think he made the right decision. I wasn't so sure at the time, but I am now."

He went on to tell Linda that it was a female, and they didn't find that out until right at last. Cork was also worried about Johnathon's condition, and he wasn't sure that Johnathon could keep going.

Cork said, "Just think a minute. If that fish gets upriver to its spawning grounds, finds a big male, and does its thing, in six or seven years, there is a possibility of some whopper Chinook salmon coming back up this river."

He went on to explain that he didn't think John could handle the fact that he had caught the world's biggest Chinook salmon, either. The publicity would be enormous. His name would be in every paper and magazine in the world, and John, as all his friends knew, was pretty much an introvert. My God, that would drive him nuts.

Linda grinned, saying, "Well, you wouldn't like it either. You two are just alike, and your name would be right there with his, in the papers and all.

"I think it would be kind of cool," she added. "Just think—years from now, our grandkids would see your name in some fishing book and be able to say, 'Hey, that's my grandpa.'" Linda wasn't just grinning now. She was laughing out loud.

"That's just fine," Cork said. "I wouldn't be around to know about it. But between now and then, life would be hell for us, and you know it. Heck, we would probably have to move and change our names."

The just made Linda laugh harder, but Cork wasn't laughing or smiling.

CHAPTER 40

Beth Roberts was twenty-three years old. She had graduated from Oregon State University the year prior, majoring in fisheries science, and she had landed her first job with the Oregon Fish and Game Commission.

It was a menial position, for sure, but it was a foot in the door, and she was proud and felt very lucky to have it.

She had applied for two positions during the winter. One was checking sport and commercial fishermen's catches during the spring and summer months and taking scale samples of their catches. It included taking pictures of their boats and anything else that was relevant.

The other opening was to walk up and down the rivers and tributaries in Northwest Oregon, generally the Tillamook County rivers, checking the spawning areas, juvenile salmon populations, predator abundance, and general habitat conditions.

The latter was the one she was chosen for. It was the position she really wanted.

Beth—who had been raised in an outdoor-loving family, which included all kinds of hunting and fishing—had just spent four years in college, where she had felt extremely confined and, at times, very bored. She had loved her classes but disliked college life to the max.

Never being the boy-crazy female like a lot of her classmates, Beth spent most of her time in her books or running back home to Salem, Oregon, to go fishing or hunting with her dad, mother, and brothers on the weekends.

Another reason she was happy with her position was that Beth had gained a considerable amount of weight during the four years in school. She knew the job required a large amount of walking up and down all types of terrain, and she planned on getting back in shape.

She had been involved in athletics during high school, and she wanted to get back to the slim and trim Beth Roberts that she used to be. She knew it would be a hard thing to do because if there was one thing she liked to do, it was to eat. She especially liked ice cream of any make or flavor and always had.

Her plan was to curb her ice cream intake—not totally, which would be impossible, but reduce it about 50 percent—and get plenty of physical exercise, which she knew she would get, walking up and down streams and rivers.

She didn't have a lot of male suitors, probably due to the weight problem and the fact that she was smarter than most males that she encountered in college. Of course, she didn't wear much makeup or tight, sexy clothes, and that didn't help.

She didn't worry too much about it. She knew the right man would come around sometime, probably some outdoorsman who was an intellectual or professor like one of her brothers. Also, her dad, who was a highly trained fisheries biologist for the federal government, would be hard to beat.

When she reported to the fish and game department's main office in Salem on her first day of work, she met her boss, Jim Leve. She was impressed with the man. Not only was he a dedicated employee, but he seemed intelligent and was good looking in a rugged, outdoorsy way.

He gave her a tour of the building, introducing her to a whole lot of people and explaining the functions of most of the various departments.

The building seemed huge to her. She had been there previously on numerous occasions, but always just to the first floor in the licensing section.

The tour lasted most of the morning and culminated at the office of the director, who was not present at that time. He was in the Portland office at a meeting and would not be back for the day. Leve told Beth that there would be plenty of time to meet him in the future.

The rest of the day was spent in Leve's office. He informed Beth what would be expected of her in her new job. He impressed upon her the importance of the conditions of salmon-spawning habitat and its relationship with the surrounding wildlife and fauna.

Her observations along the streams and rivers would be used in several different programs in the department pertaining to predicting salmon runs in the future and the health of the environment in general.

While they were talking, a young man walked into the office and sat down in an empty chair. Leve looked over and then said to Beth, "I would like you to meet one of your new partners, Scott Dale."

Dale never smiled. He just glanced at Beth and nodded and then, looking back at Leve, said, "When you get done with her, boss, I'd like to get going. We still have to load our equipment."

Leve, not smiling and with a rather gruff tone in his voice, told him to leave and start loading by himself, and he would send Beth down when they were finished.

Dale got up and, without saying anything further, left the room.

Leve sat at his desk without moving or saying anything for a few moments. Then, turning to Beth, he said, "I'm sorry for Scott's actions. I don't think he was taught many manners while he was growing up. He's not very good at conversing with other people, but he's excellent in his job."

He went on to tell Beth to listen to what Scott said and learn from him but not to pay much attention to how he said it. He really didn't intend to be such a butt; it was just who he was.

They both smiled and chuckled, but Beth sure hoped she wouldn't get into it with Scott. Sometimes Beth had a short fuse, and she knew it. She didn't take rudeness kindly from any person, no matter who they were.

The next morning when Beth arrived at the building, Scott was waiting for her. He told her that they were in a hurry to finish loading and head out to one of the coastal rivers.

He informed her that they wouldn't get much work done today—mostly instruction on what to do and where to do it.

As they were putting the last bags of equipment in the older pickup belonging to Scott, he started telling her all the dos and don'ts. One was that they were going to be walking on a lot of private property as well as US Forest Service land, and, if possible, they would contact the owner beforehand. Sometimes it wasn't possible, and watch out for dogs and electric fences.

He said, "Remember, we're only there to see and record things to do with salmon habitat, which includes about everything within twenty or thirty feet from the water's edge that affects the flow of water or could affect the flow of water. Of course, you want to take notice of anything in the water and stream bed, as you've already been told, including signs of predators and small fish that you observe."

While Scott talked, Beth noticed a certain amount of hostility in his voice, as if he didn't like her or was mad at something.

Beth was not a timid individual or someone to beat around the bush about something that bothered her, so after Scott quit talking and a brief period of silence, she looked over at him. He was behind the steering wheel, driving and looking down the road. She asked him,

"Scott, are you angry with me or mad at something I should know about?"

Scott, having not been close to any female in his life with the exception of his mother, was caught totally off guard. He had had a few brief encounters or dates in college, but nothing that had lasted. And he had talked with many females while working for the department, but nothing of a personal nature. It wasn't that he didn't like the opposite sex. He did, but he didn't consider himself very good looking, and girls didn't seem attracted to him. In other words, Scott was rather shy around girls, but he didn't want anyone to know that, especially this girl sitting in the front seat of his pickup with him right now.

He didn't know how to answer, so he just looked straight ahead while his eyes got a little large and his face got red.

He was silent for a noticeable few seconds and then, clearing his throat, answered rather quietly, "No."

Neither of them said anything, and then Scott added, "It's just that I had a hard time getting this job with the department five years ago, and I know a lot of people that I went to school with that are still getting turned down, and you walk right in and get a position on your first try."

He went on to say that he had read her resume and it was good, but it didn't show any higher qualifications than others. So he assumed she got the position because of her dad, who was highly recognized in the Federal Fish and Wildlife Service.

There was a brief period of silence before Beth said, "Well, you're probably right, but I didn't have anything to do with it—believe me, I didn't—but I do feel lucky to have the job opportunity. And I will try my best, and I would like for us to get along."

Scott, feeling a little berated, just nodded his head and continued looking down the highway. He uttered silently, "Good enough."

Not much was said between them for the next thirty or forty miles except pleasantries and observations of their surroundings.

CHAPTER 41

Coming to Hebo, which was a short distance from Nestucca River, Scott asked Beth if she had ever been there before. Beth answered, "Oh, yes, many times. I've fished on the Nestucca with my family for many years."

He pulled into the Nestucca Valley Sporting Goods Store parking lot and said, "Let's run in here and grab a cup of coffee."

Beth, who was a little carsick from the crooked highway coming over the coastal range, immediately agreed.

Pat, the owner, seeing the Fish and Wildlife Department patches on their coats and recognizing Scott, greeted them and asked where were they headed to on this day.

Beth looked at Scott as he said, "The upper river, probably Moon Creek and East Creek area. We haven't been up in that area this year yet."

After discussing the weather and how cruddy it had been and how much rain was expected in the immediate future, Scott and Beth were walking out the door when Scott turned back to Pat and said, "We'll be back later today for one of those hamburgers like I had last year."

Pat, smiling, waved and closed the door behind them.

Scott drove north on Highway 101, and when they reached the next small town, which was named Beaver, he turned right on Blaine Road. After about seven miles, they came to a junction and a small bridge called Blaine. He turned left on a road paralleling a small creek, which he told Beth was named Moon Creek.

He said that they would be working on two Nestucca tributaries, Moon Creek and East Creek, for the next couple of days. He added that historically they had been known for salmon and steelhead spawning streams.

After traveling about one-quarter of a mile, they came to another fork in the road, and Scott turned right onto a road that traveled along a creek that ran into Moon Creek. Scott told Beth that this creek was called East Creek, and he was going to drop her off in about a mile and that she was to work her way down the creek and meet him at the junction.

It took Beth almost two hours to reach the junction of the two creeks and the road. Scott was not there yet. He was still up working in the headwaters of Moon Creek.

When he finally drove up, he looked exhausted. He explained to her that after walking the creek for about a mile, he had to hike back up to relay his vehicle down.

He then worked another mile and repeated the process. Walking back to the vehicle was the hardest part; it was all uphill.

He told Beth that he wasn't feeling too good at his stomach and asked her if she would work the short distance down to Blaine, on Moon Creek, and he would drive down and wait for her. He explained that he still had one or two miles above them on Moon Creek to finish the next day.

Of course, she agreed, and out the vehicle she went.

As Scott drove off, it started to rain, hard. It had been raining off and on all day, and it looked like all the creeks and the main river had started to rise, as if they weren't high as it was. It had been an unusually wet year on the Oregon coast. The coast got a lot of rain in winter anyway, but this year it seemed to be raining every day, and the rivers had been swollen and unfishable most of the time.

It made it miserable for the salmon and steelhead fishermen, and it didn't help the sporting goods dealers and stores who were trying to make a living, either.

CHAPTER 42

Beth was having a hard time walking down the small creek. She kept having to detour around brush and trees because the water was so high. It wasn't too muddy, and she could see the bottom out from the shore for about two feet. No doubt the visibility was going to get worse with all the rain that was coming down.

Walking around some blackberry bushes on the stream's edge, she noticed some white bones lying on a gravel bar, partly hidden by some brush and debris.

She stepped down on the gravel and walked toward them. It wasn't uncommon to see salmon carcasses along the streams' bank's this time of year. In fact, that was one of the reasons she was there—to count and examine them.

As she got closer, she didn't think it was a salmon because of the size. All she could see was some backbone in the shallows, and it appeared to be too big for a fish.

Having her hip boots on, which was standard apparel for this job, she waded out to the bones. She reached down into the water, grabbed them, and tried to pull them out of the muddy debris.

It wasn't working at first, so she waded back out of the water onto the gravel bar and laid down the bag that contained her equipment so she could get a better grip on the bones.

Seeing a large stick lying on the bank, she took it out and tried to dislodge the bones with it.

This time the backbone moved a little. But it was so big, she couldn't get a good hold on it, and it kept sliding out of her hands.

Finally, using the stick again, she got it to start to come out. But the water was so muddy from her digging, she couldn't see the other end of it.

She dropped the stick and pulled with all her might, and two things happened at once: an enormous, partly dissolved fish tail came to the surface, and she slipped and fell back on her butt in the water.

She was so surprised, she just sat there in about a foot of water and stared at the backbone between her knees and the tail lying behind her feet.

There was still some skin on the tail, and she could tell it was a Salmon, but what a salmon! She had never heard of a salmon tail that big, let alone seen one.

Coming to her senses, she let go of the backbone, which was a piece about four feet long, not including the tail. She tried to stand up, which was a little difficult since her hip boots were partially full of water.

She got up, walked over to a downed log on the bank, sat down, and took her boots off to empty them, all the time staring at the fish bones that were still in the water. She still couldn't believe what she was looking at.

After taking her socks off and wringing the water out of them, she looked all around. Deciding that no one could see her, she took her Levi's off and tried to get as much water out of them as she could also.

She hurriedly put everything back on because it was really starting to rain now, and she was getting cold.

She went back into the water, grabbed the backbone with both hands, and tried to drag it up onto the gravel bar.

It was a lot heavier than she had thought it would be. She said a few choice words under her breath as she pulled, but she could only get about one foot of the backbone onto the bare gravel. Beth stood up, with her hands on her hips, and said, out loud this time, "Damn, it must weigh fifty pounds or more."

Beth had pulled deer out of the woods with her dad and had caught many salmon and steelhead in the past, and she could pretty much guess something's weight.

She was flabbergasted, and she was at a loss as to what to do next.

She went back to her pack and got out her camera. If nothing else, she was going to get a picture of the tail before she left. But then, when setting the camera, she found the battery dead. Beth dropped the camera back in her pack sack, threw her hands up in the air, stomped up and down a couple times, and said out loud again, "What is going to happen next? Damn, my first day on the job."

She then went back to her pack and dug out her tape measure, thinking, "At least I can write the measurements down so it can be recorded. I'll make sure the camera has a full charge tomorrow."

First, she measured the tail from bottom to top, at the ends, which was hard to do since they were about one to two feet underwater.

She put a rock on the end of the tape at one end of the tail and then, keeping the tape out of the water, held it above the other end. It didn't work very well, so she walked out of the water and found a long tree limb that had fallen on the ground.

With about five feet of the limb, she waded back out to the tail and held it underwater to get her measurement. And then, holding her thumbnail on the length, she walked out onto the gravel bar, got her tape back out, and ran it from the end to her thumbnail. It measured a little over two feet, eight inches, or thirty-two inches.

She stood there looking down the creek for a minute and thinking, Absolutely no one is going to believe this. I have to get back here tomorrow and get a picture. And then, she thought, Maybe Scott has a camera. He should have one in his pack.

It was really raining hard now. Beth, even with her raincoat and hat, was soaked to the bone. She tried shielding her notepad with her body so she could record her measurements, but it just wouldn't work.

Finally, she decided to wait until she got into Scott's vehicle, out of the rain, to try to write down the measurement.

CHAPTER 43

She crawled up the bank from the gravel bar and started walking downstream. It wasn't far to the Blaine Road junction, where the creek ran into the big river, but she thought she should thoroughly check the rest of the creek for some more of the fish's carcass and anything else of note before going to Scott's vehicle.

It was really raining hard, and she kept slipping on the steep bank. She could see that the creek was getting muddy, and when she got to the vehicle, which Scott had parked in a large turnout just below the junction, she could see that the Nestucca was getting darker in color too.

Before she opened the passenger door, she could see that Scott was lying back in his seat, apparently asleep. With the noise of the door opening, he slowly turned toward her and said, "Boy, that took longer than I thought it would. What took you so long?" And then, seeing she was soaked as she took her raincoat off and pulled her hip boots down, he added, "My God, Beth. Did you fall in the creek or something?"

As she jumped into the seat, fast, getting out of the rain, she took a good look at him and asked, "You look awful. Are you sick?"

Scott was pale as a sheet and had been sick at his stomach since he had dropped her off. He told her so as he started the engine and said, "Maybe one of Pat's hamburgers will make me feel better—that is, if he's still open."

Beth told him to wait, that she wanted to borrow his camera because her camera's batteries were dead, and she wanted to go back up the creek to take a picture of something.

Scott told her that it would have to wait until the next day because of the storm. It was getting dark, and he just didn't feel good enough to hang around any longer.

He wanted to know what she had found that she had to take a picture of. He voiced his concern about wanting to get back out in the storm to do anything, much less trying to take a picture.

Not only did it seem like it was raining harder, but now the wind was blowing, and the rain was going sideways.

Beth, reluctant to say anything, casually said, "Oh, there's a half of a fish carcass I wanted to take a picture of to show you and Jim. I guess it'll just have to wait until tomorrow, like you said."

The subject was dropped on the twenty-minute drive to Hebo. All they could talk about was the storm that was blowing leaves and small tree limbs across the road in front of them.

The sporting goods store was still open when they got to Hebo, and three vehicles were in the parking lot in front of the store. Scott told Beth that he thought it was unusual for the store to have that many customers that time of day. But, on the other hand, nobody could be fishing in the storm, so they were probably in the store drinking coffee and telling fishing stories.

Cork was in the store when Beth and Scott walked in. He had driven over from his home in the valley to deliver some fishing bobbers and other gear that Pat had ordered.

Cork made various kinds of bait and lures that he sold to Pat and other sporting goods stores, and since the weather was so poor and he couldn't go fishing or work outside, he had decided to make some deliveries that he had been putting off.

He was bent down, looking at some fishing equipment and talking to a couple of locals who were sitting behind him at one of the deli's tables, when the door opened and a blast of air rushed in with the two fish and game employees. Pat, who was behind the counter, close to the door, immediately grabbed it and shut it behind them.

Everybody in the room started laughing and talking at once about the lousy weather and fishing except Cork, who, with his back still to the whole group, was intently studying a fishing lure.

Scott asked Pat if it was too late to order a couple of hamburgers. Pat said, "Of course not" and walked to the back of the store to tell the cook, who was still there preparing some of the next day's menu.

Meanwhile, Scott and Beth took off their raincoats, and, after each got a cup of coffee, they sat down at the last empty table.

One of the customers asked out loud, "What is so important that a couple of fish and game people would be out in this weather?"

Scott informed him that they had been up on Moon Creek making a walking survey of the stream's salmon-rearing capabilities and condition from last year's storms and high water, noting any pertinent information involving evidence of last year's salmon run in general.

The man, known for being kind of a smartass, said, "We would have a lot more fish in those streams if you guys hadn't done away with the hatch box program a few years ago."

Cork stopped what he was doing and looked back at the man who had made the statement, and then he noticed that Pat was watching him, probably hoping that Cork wouldn't say something on the subject and get into an argument with the guy. Cork didn't like the man, and Pat knew it. Pat didn't care much for him either. In fact, Cork had heard that Pat had kicked the guy out of his shop one time, but Pat never would talk about it much.

Cork knew a little about the hatch box program, although he never did operate one. It gave private people and organizations the opportunity to raise fish in a boxlike affair constructed of wire, from eggs that were given to them from the Fish and Game Commission. When the fish reached fingerling size and were ready to spend their year in freshwater before migrating downstream to the ocean, they were released, and nature took over.

The whole process was overseen by the commission, of course, and seemed to be quite efficient and productive. The commission did away with the program a few years back for some reason that Cork didn't know about, but he figured it was probably lack of funds or something involving competition with native stock, which was usually the case.

Anyway, there were a lot of hard feelings left over, and the subject would come up all the time when a group of sports fishermen and landowners met employees of the commission, whether in public meetings or accidental meetings such as in sporting goods stores.

CHAPTER 44

Scott, who had probably heard this allegation several times previously, handled it very gracefully, stating how the salmon spawning stocks seemed to be holding their own and that a person never knew what might come up in future. He went on to say how there were larger Chinook salmon caught last season than in previous years. He didn't know why, but he thought it was a good thing.

Beth listened very intently and then said, "Yes, we're seeing evidence of some very large fish. I just saw a tail of a spawned-out carcass that measured two feet, eight inches from top to bottom. It must have been a really big fish when it was alive."

A whole lot of things happened at once. Chairs squeaked as men moved and sat up straight, a couple of men coughed, and Cork dropped the lure he was looking at and turned around, still bent over. Every man in the room was looking at Beth with eyes wide, including Scott.

Suddenly, every person in the room started laughing—all but Cork. His eyes were wide, and his mind was working miles a minute. Then he started laughing and asked, "Where in the world did you see that?"

Beth, who wasn't laughing, answered, "On Moon Creek, just above Blaine."

Scott had stopped laughing now and was looking Beth in the eye and shaking his head, trying to stop her from saying any more. But Beth, who didn't like being laughed at, started to turn red with a little humiliation and continued telling the group how she had tried to pull it up on a gravel bar. But it was too heavy, so she measured it under about one foot of water.

Now, most of the men were bent over with tears in their eyes from laughing so hard, visualizing this little young wisp of a woman standing, bent over in the water, trying to measure a salmon tail that by her description was as big as a small whale.

Finally, things started to calm down. The men quit laughing so hard. Other people had come into the store and were asking what the calamity was all about. And, of course, the loudmouth was taking front stage and telling them what Beth had said.

One of the women who had come in asked no one in particular, "What was so funny about that?" with a calm and inquisitive look on her face.

That did it. All the men who were sitting down at the tables quickly looked into one another's eyes and started laughing all over again.

After about five minutes, things started to calm down again. Pat brought Scott and Beth's hamburgers and, as he served them, he noticed that Cork was gone. He hadn't see him leave. He thought that it was rather strange, because he hadn't given him a check for the bobbers and lures that he had brought, and Cork never left without getting paid.

Pat looked outside in the parking lot for Cork's pickup but couldn't see it, so that meant Cork had headed back home. Pat wondered if he was all right and then turned back to his customers.

The store was full of people, which usually happened when a big storm suddenly came into the area. Everybody tried to get out of the weather.

Of course, the customers were still talking about Beth's measurement of the spawned Chinook salmon's tail.

After the loudmouth's accusation that Beth had better take a college class in measuring things underwater and Scott's constant kicking her under the table when she started to make a comment, she finally said that she must have made a mistake.

It took a lot out of Beth to do this. She had probably never admitted that she was wrong more than two or three times in her entire life. She was a very calculating and precise individual, and she just didn't say or do things that she wasn't sure of.

Scott and Beth finished their meal, paid Pat, and were starting out the door when a small voice in the back of the crowd could be heard saying, "I would give her a lesson on how to use a tape measure anytime." That started some more snickers and laughing.

Beth stopped with a stone look on her face and was going to turn around, but Scott grabbed her by the arm, and, with a shake of his head, led her out door.

When they got to Scott's vehicle, Beth, red faced and getting more pissed off by the second, jumped into the passenger seat and slammed the door.

Scott was rather fearful of what was coming because he had never been capable of handling irate females—not that he had had much experience at it except for family members, but it didn't take an expert to see that there was one sitting in his front seat.

As soon as he sat down and closed the door, Beth was in his face. She wanted to know what was with all the kicking her under the table and pulling her out the door before she could answer those idiots at the tables. She added that if her shins were bruised, she was going to inform one of her brothers, and he would probably put a bruise or two on him.

She went on to inform Scott she knew exactly what she was doing and could use a tape measure quite expertly, and, in fact, that was a true measurement she had taken. The tail measured thirty-two inches.

Beth went on to say that she was aware that it was big and she should never have blurted it out in front of those idiots, but she was just backing him up about what he had said about larger salmon in last year's run.

She was talking very fast and loud, and Scott couldn't get a word in even if he wanted to. He just sat there with eyes big and mouth shut and took the verbal abuse.

Finally, he started the engine and proceeded to drive away from the store, hoping that none of the people in there had heard or seen what was going on in his vehicle.

Unbeknownst to him, some of the customers had opened the store door to leave when Beth and Scott were in their vehicle, and most of the people had not only heard but had seen Beth lose her temper.

When Scott circled around the store from the parking lot and drove in front, most of the customers were standing outside, bending over in laughter while Beth was still telling him what she thought of him.

When Beth saw the people, she looked back and forth at Scott and the store a couple of times. Calming down somewhat as Scott turned onto the highway to Salem and the valley, she asked, "Oh my God, did those idiots hear me?"

Scott said, "What do you think?"

After traveling for two or three miles, Beth uttered a feeble "I'm sorry, but I don't like to be made fun of and called a liar or told that I don't know how to use a stupid tape measure. I did measure that tail correctly, and it was thirty-two inches from the top to the bottom."

Scott, in control of himself after the store incident, said rather loudly, "That's bullshit, Beth, and you know it. There is no salmon of any species known to man that has a tail that size. I don't have to tell you that. Why did you tell all those fishermen something like that? Now we're going to be the laughingstock in this whole area, and we'll be lucky if it doesn't reach headquarters, and I would sure like to see you explain what you said to Jim or maybe even the director."

Beth, getting mad all over again, sat silently for a couple of seconds and then turned her head toward Scott. With eyes blazing, she said, "OK, turn this damned car around and go back up to Blaine. I'm going to show you that tail, and I expect a big 'I'm sorry' when this is all over."

"Now, you are really acting crazy," Scott said. "In the first place, this storm, if it isn't bad enough, is supposed to get worse, according to Pat. And it's almost dark now. When we get to Blaine, it will be totally dark. And secondly, I still don't feel good. I must be catching something. I don't want to be crawling up and down a creek bank and getting soaked."

He paused and then added, "Besides, we got all day tomorrow."

Scott quit talking, thought for a minute, and then said, "Beth, you are entering a field of work that involves men, a lot of men. Probably 75 percent of the fishermen and hunters in this state are male, and this is just occurring in the last ten or twenty years. Before that there were very few women who hunted or picked up a fishing pole.

"Now, you must remember, most of the money our department runs on comes from these people, so public relations is a major factor.

"That voice you heard teasing you about learning how to use a measuring tape back in Pat's store was not referring to the fish's tail but something more personal. I'm sure that if you think a minute, you can figure out.

"A woman working around these sometimes-macho male individuals must learn to let comments like that go in one ear and out the other, especially a good-looking female like you." Scott could see, out of the corner of his eye, Beth go rigid and kind of bristle up, like she was going to explode.

He thought that maybe he had made a mistake in talking like that to her. After all, he really wasn't her supervisor. Jim was, and it was Jim's responsibility to explain these things, not his.

Beth, finally visibly calming somewhat, said, "Scott, I want to ask you something."

Scott thought, Well, here it comes. I've had it now.

After a short pause and Scott telling her to go ahead, Beth asked, "Do you really think I'm good looking?"

Beth had just put Scott into a field that he knew little if anything about. He didn't answer right away; he just stammered a little. His eyes seemed to get a little bigger, and his face was gradually and visibly turning red.

Beth had just turned the tables on Scott. He thought his discourse on the measuring-tape episode had crossed the line and embarrassed her. It didn't. It had just pissed her off.

If Scott had known her better, he would not have tried it. Beth may have not had much experience being up close with men, but she was quite worldly, having been raised by an almost-all-male family, with exception of her mother. And she could ask her mother anything—and that means anything—about men, and her mother would tell her, sometimes in a rather rough way. Her mother and she were very close.

Scott finally got out that yes, he thought she was good looking, and nothing more was said on that subject the rest of the way to Salem.

If Scott would have looked closely at Beth, which he couldn't, he would have seen that she had a twinkle in her eyes and a smirky smile on her lips.

On the way home, she thought if he would have let her answer that loudmouth idiot in the store, she would have really put him in his place. She would have said something like they don't make tape measures that small for people with such small brains. She would have hesitated before she got out the word "brains." She was sure all the people in the store would have had a big laugh at that.

Occasionally, she would glance over at Scott and tell herself, "He's not so bad looking. Not at all." And her smile got a little bigger.

CHAPTER 45

After Cork's initial shock at hearing what Beth said in the sporting goods store and while everyone was laughing, he quietly walked around everybody and out the door to his pickup.

He then drove around the back of the store and turned up the highway heading to the valley. He didn't think anyone would notice him leaving, not knowing that Pat had. Of course, Pat didn't miss much of anything happening around his store.

When Cork got to the turnoff toward Mt. Hebo, he went up the road heading to John's house.

He was excited and going too fast. He made himself slow down before he slid off the road going around some turn, which there was no shortage of on the Mount Hebo Road, and the storm just made it worse.

Reaching Johnathon's house, he drove into the driveway and hit his brakes.

The lights in the house were on, so that meant that someone was home. Hopefully, John.

As he ran up to the back door, it opened, and Lucy was standing there with a surprised look on her face. She hadn't seen him drive up.

Cork asked her where John was, and she motioned toward the garage, telling him that was where she was headed when he drove up.

Cork followed her into the garage, where Johnathon was bent over his boat trailer, working on the hitch.

Johnathon looked over at him and said, "I thought I heard your pickup come in. What's up?"

Cork excitedly told Johnathon to grab his hip boots and a couple of large garbage bags, if he had any, that a fish and game girl had found part of a large spawned-out salmon carcass up on Moon Creek, and they were going to go get it.

Johnathon stopped what he was doing and just looked at Cork and then asked, "Are you crazy or something? Why in the hell would we want to go out in this storm for a salmon carcass?"

Cork said, "Because she said she measured its tail, and it was thirty-two inches from top to bottom. That's why."

"Oh, hell, there is no salmon in the world with a tail that big," Johnathon said. And then he stopped appearing to be thinking and added, "Except maybe one."

He dropped a wrench that he had in his hand, and it went clattering on the cement floor as he quickly jumped up and walked to a shelf that had his hip boots hanging on it.

After grabbing the boots and his raincoat, which was hanging next to them, he grabbed a box of large black garbage bags and headed for the door, saying, "Let's go."

Lucy, who had been listening, said, "You two are going to catch your death of pneumonia out in weather like this. Why don't you wait until tomorrow. Maybe it won't be storming so bad."

As Johnathon walked by her in the doorway, he bent to the side, kissed her on the forehead, and, with a grin, muttered, "A man's got to do what a man's got to do, hon. We'll be back before too long."

Lucy just stood there and shook her head as they drove off. She waved, smiled, and said in a low voice, "You two old fools." And then she laughed out loud as they went out of sight.

CHAPTER 46

On the way to Blaine, Cork told Johnathon everything he had heard the girl say in the sporting goods store. He figured that she must have meant the gravel bar that can be partially seen from Moon Creek Road, about one hundred yards above the junction of Moon Creek and the Nestucca River.

Johnathon agreed, because that was about the only place she could wade in that area with the water up so high.

When they got to the area, Johnathon jumped out, and Cork turned around and went back to Blaine and parked his pickup in a large area off the road. Then he walked back up the creek to Johnathon.

He found Johnathon out in the water, hanging on to some brush. There was no gravel bar visible because the water had probably come up a good foot since Scott and Beth had been there.

Cork found a large limb lying on the bank and waded out to where Johnathon was feeling around with his feet underwater. He started pushing the limb out as far as he could reach but never felt any obstruction.

When Cork worked his way downstream, almost to where some brush was hanging in the water, he felt something with his limb. He yelled over to Johnathon, who was only twenty or twenty-five feet away. But it was raining so hard, it was difficult for them to hear each other.

Johnathon came over to Cork. They were in almost to the top of their boots. Cork pulled in the limb and busted off a small limb that was sticking out from the main one, making a small hook. Then he put it back out as far as he could reach and pushed to the bottom and then started to pull it in. It caught on something, and Cork, with Johnathon's help, started to pull it up.

They could see that it was a piece of salmon carcass, but when it got about four feet from them, it slid off the limb and started to sink.

Johnathon, without thinking, made a wild grab for it and went underwater. He came back up with it in both hands and yelled to Cork for help.

Cork, who was just getting up out of the water himself, had been pulling hard on the limb because of the weight of the carcass and the strong current when the carcass came off. He lost his balance and fell backward in the water when Johnathon made the wild grab for the bones.

Cork grabbed Johnathon by the shoulders of his coat and started to pull back. He wasn't getting anywhere at first because of the current, and Johnathon was mostly underwater.

Finally, he started to inch backward toward where he figured the shallowest area was.

Johnathon, still having ahold of the fish carcass with both hands, was coughing and sputtering that he had swallowed a gallon of water. And although Cork was doing most of the work, at least he was staying upright.

Cork didn't answer him. He was having too much trouble. He had lost his footing several times, and he was running out of strength. He was afraid that if he lost his footing again, they might both go into the main current. And with the hip boots they had on...well, it wouldn't be good.

They got into the shallower area, where the water was just below their waist and wasn't as swift. Johnathon was helping now, and pulling back was easier on Cork, although he had to turn sideways and vomit from the exertion just as they got to the shoreline.

They were still in water over their boots, but they stopped to rest before going any farther. Johnathon, catching his breath, said, "This damned fish is going to kill us yet. I hope you know that."

They both looked at each other and started laughing.

Cork said, "Well, I'll tell you one thing: We're getting way too old to be doing this shit. Hell, we were too old thirty years ago to be doing this.

"This is your fault, you know? If you had kept this damned fish when you caught it in the first place, we wouldn't be doing this. Hell, John, you would be a celebrity by now. Everyone would know your name. Probably even have your picture and name on a Wheaties box as the world's best salmon fisherman."

"Cork, you are still an asshole. And, by the way, your picture and name would be right beside mine. I would make sure of that."

And then Johnathon added, "By the way, I need to get out of this water. My feet are turning numb, so let's see if we can get these bones up on the bank while I can still walk."

Cork stopped laughing, let go of Johnathon, reached around in front of him, grabbed the backbone just below his hands, and said, "OK, let's go for it."

They dragged the bones up onto the bank, which was no easy task, and sat down, both breathing hard.

Johnathon said, "Good grief. I'll bet the creek has come up six inches since we got here."

Looking back and down at the waterline, Cork said, "I think you're right. We'd better drag this thing up by the road before I go and get the pickup."

Getting the bones up the bank was a major task because not only was it about forty feet, but steep, and it was raining so hard the men couldn't keep from slipping.

Finally, they made it. While Cork took off for the vehicle, Johnathon lay down on the ground next to the road beside the bones.

Johnathon heard a vehicle stop down by the bridge and junction where Cork was probably getting into his pickup.

He grabbed the partial carcass and pulled it into some high grass to hide it from view—at least he hoped it would.

He heard the vehicle coming up the road, and he sat down on part of the tail, trying to further conceal it.

The small pickup slowly came up the road and stopped by Johnathon. A man rolled his driver's-side window down and, smiling, said, "John, what the dickens are you doing out here, sitting down in the grass beside the road in a storm like this? You must be getting a little foolish in your old age, huh?" The man then started laughing, loud.

The man's name was Mel, and he lived just up Moon Creek Road about a mile. Both Cork and Johnathon had known Mel for about thirty years. He was retired from working for the Fish and Game Commission at the local fish hatchery.

Johnathon, looking up at him, didn't know quite what to say, so he blurted out, "Cork and I decided to take a walk up here on the road, and I got tuckered out. So, Cork went to get the pickup. You know I have a bad ticker and all."

Mel just grinned and looked at Johnathon for a second or two and then asked, "Did you find that dead fish you were looking for?"

Johnathon was getting flustered and pissed off. He figured that Cork had told him something entirely different. Getting red in face, he asked rather loudly, "Mel, what is this third degree I'm getting? Can't a guy sit down next to the road anymore?"

"Now John, don't get all upset. I'm just having a little fun. I don't really care what you guys are doing up here as long as you're OK," Mel said. He then added, "When Cork gets here and picks you up, which should be any minute, why don't you two come on up to the house for a cup of coffee?"

Johnathon, calming down, said rather sheepishly, "We'll think on it. I'll mention it to Cork when he gets here."

Mel, thinking he had better not say any more, nodded his head and drove off. As he was leaving, he took off his hat and scratched his head, thinking, Those two old coots are up to something. He laughed out loud and thought, They should have got their stories straight. And then he laughed some more as he turned into his driveway.

CHAPTER 47

Cork drove up and stopped in the middle of road because there was no pullout. He jumped out with the two garbage sacks and ran to Johnathon, who was still sitting down in the grass on part of the fish carcass.

Cork immediately asked, "Are you all right? What are you doing, sitting down in the wet grass in this rain?"

Johnathon said, "What did you tell Mel? He acted like I was crazy when I told him we had gone for a walk up the road and you went back to get your pickup because I pooped out."

Cork stopped what he was doing and looked over at John. He grinned and said, "Good Lord. I told him the truth and said we were looking for a fish carcass in Moon Creek, but I didn't say any more than that. He probably thinks we're idiots or lying to him, or probably both.

"Come on, John. Get up, and let's get that thing in the bags and in the back of the pickup and get out of here."

Johnathon stood up, and they got the carcass in the bags and loaded. Of course, it didn't all fit in the bags, so they covered it up as well as they could, trying to get out of the middle of the road before Mel came back or somebody else came along.

As they were traveling down Blain Road, Cork looked over at Johnathon and noticed he was as pale as a sheet and shaking all over. He turned the heat up in the vehicle all the way.

After about five minutes, Johnathon started looking a lot better. He said, "Cork, I've got to quit doing crap like that. It's my heart. Doctor said that I don't have a long time so to be a little careful. I feel better now, but I was feeling a little poorly there for a while."

Cork's eyes got big, and he immediately slowed down the vehicle. He said, "When did this all happen, and why didn't you tell me, John? For God's sake, you shouldn't even be out here."

"That's the reason I didn't tell you, damn it," said Johnathon. "I don't plan on changing anything in my life much. I want to live like I always have, and I don't plan on dying in bed. You know how I feel about this. We've talked about it before, and you feel the same way."

Cork didn't say anything for about five minutes, and then he said, "I totally understand, John. But from now on, we're going to do things a little different. Well, maybe different isn't the right word. We're going to slow down a bit and not go to extremes like we just did. Hell, we didn't need those damn bones anyhow. I just wanted something to prove that we actually did what we did. I mean, we didn't even get a picture of the fish."

Johnathon said, "What are we going to do with those bones? We can take pictures of them, but they'll just lie around, rot, and draw flies. And besides, they might not be from our fish, anyway."

Cork looked over at Johnathon. "Come on, John. They're from your fish, and you know it. There's no other Chinook salmon that big, and never has been. And as far as that goes, probably never will be.

"Now, I've got plans for that fish's tail. I'll take it home with me so you aren't pestered by the flies and such. God forbid, I wouldn't want it lying around your yard stinking like your boat does half the time."

Johnathon looked over at Cork with a slight grin and said, "There you go, being an asshole again. I like the idea of you taking them to the valley. It was your idea to go get them in the first place."

Both men were quiet for a minute, and then Johnathon said, "By the way, we both darn near drowned a while ago. I hope you realize that. I don't know about you, but tonight before I go to bed, I'm going to add an extra note of thanks when I talk to the man above."

Johnathon looked down at his lap and was fidgeting with his fingers. "I don't know where you mustered up the strength to hold me in that current, but if you had let go, I would have been a goner. With my hip boots full of water, I would have gone to the bottom under that brush."

Cork didn't say anything. He knew what had almost happened. One time he had slipped and almost went down but somehow got his footing again. This wasn't the first time in his life that he figured he had gotten some help from above. He would never have let John go, though, no matter what happened.

They arrived at Johnathon's house, and nothing further was said on that topic.

Lucy ran out to the vehicle as it drove into the driveway, holding an umbrella over her head because it was still raining hard.

One look at Johnathon as he got out of the pickup, and she went into her normal routine of acting totally disgusted with him, telling him to get to the garage and out of all those wet clothes and boots and then into the shower.

Johnathon didn't say a word. He just waved at Cork as he walked toward the garage.

Lucy pointed her finger at Cork and was going to say something as he backed out the driveway. Smiling, he waved out the window, yelled, "See ya, Luce," and drove away, thinking, Wow, is he in for it or what.

CHAPTER 48

Scott dropped Beth off at her parents' house after they reached Salem. The storm had gotten there before them and was in full swing as Beth, after saying good-bye to Scott, tried to get from the vehicle to the house without getting drenched again. Not that she was totally dry from her experience on Moon Creek, but at least she was warm.

Scott had told her that he would meet up with her again at headquarters the next morning, and they would head out to the Nestucca again.

Beth's mother, after hearing a vehicle in the driveway, met Beth at the door and, seeing how wet she was, made her strip and give up her clothes before coming any farther. Beth headed for the shower, and her mother took the clothes to the laundry room. As they parted, her mother informed her in a rather harsh voice that she would probably catch something from being wet so long and that when she finished in the shower to come to the kitchen and get something hot to drink. Beth, who never argued with her mother, agreed to do so.

While Beth was washing and getting dry clothes on, her thoughts drifted to Scott. He didn't believe her measurement of the fish's tail, and she knew it. It was rather big for a salmon, no doubt, but she hadn't made a mistake. She would prove it to him the next day. She would make him measure it himself.

The carcass was a salmon. It could be no other species that she was aware of. She had seen many other salmon dead along the creeks and riverbanks that day, which was not unusual because spawning season had been over for a month or more.

Most of the salmon carcasses that she could identify were Chinook, although one of them could have been a coho, which she entered on the report form that she filled out.

Beth got dressed and headed downstairs to the kitchen. It was well past suppertime, and she wondered where her father was. She hadn't noticed him when she came in, and he was usually home by this time every day during the week.

When she asked her mother, she was informed that he had received a call from a friend at the Oregon Fish and Game Headquarters just moments ago, as he walked through the door, and he had gone down to meet with him.

He had told her mother that she and Beth should go ahead and start supper without him, and he would be back as soon as possible, which they did because Beth was famished.

Just as Beth was finishing, her father walked in, took off his coat, greeted his wife and daughter, and sat down at the table. As Beth's mother got up to dish up his plate from the kitchen, he looked over at Beth, smiled, and was silent for a couple of seconds. And then he said, "My God, girl, what have you done? You started a commotion down at the fish and game that is unreal." He then laughed and added, "Not bad for your first day at work."

Before Beth could say anything, he told her that when he arrived, he could hear shouting from the parking lot, and when he walked up to the second floor, it was a madhouse. He heard words like "liar," "totally mistaken," and "just a young girl." They quieted somewhat when they saw him walk in, probably because about half of them recognized him.

He said that apparently, her partner, a Scott somebody, had gone into Jim's office and showed him her recorded paper work for the day, which included the measurement of a Salmon carcass whose tail was thirty-two inches from top to bottom.

Jim, who was a close friend of Beth's dad, tried to get Scott to explain the circumstances and what had happened for Beth to come up with a story like that.

Scott became extremely flustered and tried to explain that nothing had happened, disregarding his history of not getting along with previous people he had worked with. Beth and he seemed to be getting along just fine.

Apparently, many people heard their conversation and spread it throughout the Fishery Division offices, so when Beth's dad arrived, the vocal conflict was in full swing.

Still looking directly at Beth, he said, "Beth, I know you probably better than anyone, and I know that you didn't make a mistake when you took the measurement and wrote it down on your survey form. But are you absolutely sure that it was a salmon?"

Beth didn't hesitate when she answered with a distinct "Yes" and then added, "I couldn't get a complete examination of the bones because they were too heavy for me to get out of the water, but I know they were a salmon. And besides, there's no way a fish that big of any other species could be up on Moon Creek."

Beth went on to say that Scott and she would return to where the bones were the next morning and bring them back to the department, and then everyone would realize that no mistake had been made.

Her dad wanted to know why they didn't go back and at least get some pictures.

Beth explained that Scott was not feeling good, and it was storming bad at the time. So they decided to wait until tomorrow.

After taking a bite of his supper, he said, "I don't think that was a good idea, Beth. You and Scott should have gone back immediately and tried to get the carcass out of the water."

"Why?"

He explained that the storm had still not let up, and if the creek water was rising at that time, probably by now the bones had been washed downstream, and they would never find them.

Beth's eyes got big, and she said, "Oh, my God. I never thought about that. And the water was pretty swift. I can't imagine what it's like now, let alone tomorrow morning."

CHAPTER 49

At seven thirty the next morning, while Beth and her parents were just finishing their breakfast, Scott drove up to their house. Beth met him halfway to the door with a questioning look on her face, and he immediately told her that he thought it would be a good idea to talk to her before they got to the office.

Beth grabbed the small pack sack that she carried instead of a purse, and they left for the Fish and Game Building while Scott explained to Beth what had happened the night before, after he had dropped her off at home.

He told her that he had expected a surprised reaction when he turned in her stream survey report, but he had not expected the turmoil it caused. They were still going at it when he left for home, about an hour later, just about the time her dad arrived.

Scott figured her dad had told her about what had gone on, but he wanted to tell her himself so she would know what to expect when they got to the department.

He went on to say that there would probably be a crowd when they got there and to expect some company on their trip to Moon Creek. He also informed her that he had not answered any questions about what she had seen. He had told them they would have to ask her for the answers, so she should expect to be swarmed on when they got there.

Scott's warning was justified, because when they got to the department's parking lot, there were people waiting for them, and they were not all fish and wildlife employees. Someone had contacted, or had at least told, a person who worked for a local newspaper, and at least two reporters and their camera crews were present. Their vans were visible, parked in the lot with the other vehicles.

Beth had never gone through anything like this before, and, not knowing what to do or say, she was apprehensive. She asked Scott to keep driving.

Scott said, "Good God, Beth, I can't do that. Jim is standing over on the side next to the director. If I don't stop, we'll probably both lose our jobs."

Beth didn't say any more. She just stared at the crowd with eyes big.

As soon as the vehicle stopped and Beth started to open the door, the questions started all at once.

"Miss Roberts, did you really see a dead salmon as big as a sea lion?" That made Beth stop, with her mouth wide open. She hesitated for a second and then said, "No, absolutely not." And then, without pausing, she headed straight for Jim, who was waving her to him with a very fast motion of his hand as he headed into the building.

He was holding the door open for her as she caught up to him, the director having already entered and disappeared.

As she got close to him, he said with a grin, "One day on the job, and it looks like you're a celebrity, Beth."

She didn't smile or answer. She just headed upstairs to his office.

Jim Leve's office was full of people, which was as frustrating to Beth as the parking area had been, although at least most, if not all, of these people worked for the fish and game department. There were specialists in three or four different fields, who, to Beth and Scott's surprise, were going to accompany them to Moon Creek.

This put Scott, who was an introvert in his own right, in a rather bad mood, and he voiced his concern to Jim, asking him if wouldn't it be better to verify the find of the fish carcass first and even bring in to one of the department's labs before all this whoop-de-do.

Jim agreed with him but said that it was out of his hands, that the director thought the department had a lack of publicity as of late, and this would do just nicely.

Scott snorted, grabbed Beth by the arm, and said, "Let's get the hell out of here." He led her back out to his vehicle.

As they were leaving the parking lot, he noticed people running for vehicles in his rearview mirror, and, as they were leaving Salem, two of the vehicles were following them.

Beth hadn't said a word since she had gotten into the vehicle, but now she looked at Scott and said, "Good

Lord, what did I do? I should never have written that measurement down on the Stream Survey Report Form. I had no idea this would happen."

She paused and added, "Scott, my dad brought something to my attention that I had not thought of. It's been raining hard for two days, and Moon Creek was rising fast before we left yesterday. There's a good chance the bones were washed downstream and we won't find them today."

The vehicle started to slow. Scott was looking straight ahead. Finally, he said, "Good Lord, I never thought about that. We should have gone back for them yesterday. This is all my fault. I didn't feel good at my stomach and just wanted to go home."

It was quiet for a minute or so, and then, gripping the steering wheel so tight that his knuckles turned white, he said, "I'm really sorry, Beth, but I think your dad was probably right. I guess we'll find out for sure in a half hour or so."

They found out sooner than expected. Coming around a corner and passing the Little Nestucca River junction, they could see Three Rivers, another tributary of the Big Nestucca River.

It was so swollen that it was flowing over its banks. Scott looked at Beth and said, "Well, I guess that answers our question, but we'll continue on to Moon Creek, just to make sure. Some areas get more rain than others."

When they went past Hebo and the sporting goods store, Pat, who was talking to Chuck Rowland—a man who, incidentally, had grown up on Moon Creek

Road—noticed Scott's vehicle, with two fish and game vehicles following, turn north on Highway 101.

He quietly said, "I wonder what they're up to today."

Chuck asked, "Who? What?"

Pat told him what had happened in his store the previous day and then added, "Apparently, this all took place on Moon Creek, up in your country."

They stood and looked at each other momentarily, and then Chuck smiled and said, "Well, I think I'll just mosey up there and see for myself, because I just talked to Mel, my old neighbor, and he said that he seen Cork and John up there yesterday evening, poking around on the creek in a suspicious manner. And you know those two. They're always up to something, good or bad." He was laughing out loud when he went out the door.

Just north of Hebo, Scott and Beth saw the Big Nestucca River for the first time that morning, and it looked bad—muddy, and in some places over its bank and into farm fields.

Scott told Beth that they were probably out of luck, but he kept on driving up the river to Moon Creek.

When they got to Blaine, where Moon Creek ran into the Big River, there was no question that the retrieval of the bones was not going to be possible.

Scott stopped the vehicle, and they both, without saying a word, sat there and looked at the river and creek. The two cars that were following them pulled over behind them, and the occupants got out and were also looking at the river.

One of drivers of the following cars walked up as Scott rolled down his window. He asked if this was the spot where Beth had measured the fish carcass, and Scott told him the location was up the creek a short distance.

Asked if they were going on up, Scott said, "No, there's no use to, since the water's come up so much that the bones have probably been washed two miles downriver, or farther, by now."

The man said that they would head back to Salem and tell everyone the bad news. He was sure the director was going to be disappointed, because he had planned a big press conference on the information—after the biologist's examination, of course.

After a short pause, he said, "It's going to be hard for people to believe that a salmon that size actually existed without evidence."

Without smiling and acting a little disgusted, the man turned around and walked back to his car, told everyone to get back in, and both cars left, going back the way they had come.

Scott muttered, more to himself than to Beth, "I don't like people much. I like pooches; they're smarter and nicer."

Beth, who had been looking out the side window at the river, turned around and stared at Scott for a second before starting to laugh. That did it. Before long, both were laughing so hard they had tears running down their cheeks.

Scott said, "Let's go back to Hebo and see what Pat has for breakfast."

As they were turning around, Chuck drove past.

Chuck, seeing the vehicles going back down the road, thought, Those game commission people do some strange things sometimes. If they drove all the way over here to look at some fish bones that Pat told me about, that they had found in the creek, after all this rain...boy, I think they should go back to school.

He decided to go on up Moon Creek and talk to Mel.

CHAPTER 50

After dropping Johnathon off at home, Cork headed over the Coastal Mountains to the Willamette Valley, where he lived.

All the way back, he thought about how he was going to preserve the tail section. He had already decided to take off a good portion of the backbone and just keep the tail. He figured the tail might look kind of cool mounted on John's wall, but Lucy would have a fit about the backbone. Besides, the tail by itself must weigh about twenty-five pounds, which was too heavy to hang on a wall, let alone the backbone, which he figured weighed at least that much.

He pulled into his driveway and parked in the carport. Linda came out of the house and met him as he got out of the pickup.

She wanted to know why it had taken him so long to deliver bobbers to Pat's, and he told her the story about the fish and wildlife people coming into the sporting goods store and talking about the big fish carcass in Moon Creek.

He also told her about how he and John had almost drowned in Moon Creek trying to get the bones out. He stopped talking after that, knowing he shouldn't have mentioned that part of the story. Linda was always getting on him about taking too many chances at his age. Oh well, he had already said it. He couldn't take it back now, and John would have told her anyway.

It was quiet for a second, and Linda was staring at Cork. She said, "Get into the house right now and get out of those clothes. You're still soaked. Look at the windows in the pickup; they're all steamed up."

Cork did as he was told. He knew better than to argue, and besides, Linda hadn't quit talking since he had gotten into the house.

When he was opening the door to the shower, she asked what he had done with the tail, and he told her it was still in the back of the pickup.

When he had finished his shower, she came rushing through the bedroom door with her eyes big, and she said, "My God, Cork, I looked at the bones. The tail is absolutely huge. Do you think that's from the salmon you guys released last fall?"

Cork told her that it almost had to be. There was no way that there could be another salmon that big anywhere in the world, let alone in the Nestucca River.

Linda thought for a minute and then said, "You know, Cork, sometimes you exaggerate a little when you talk about fishing—no, sometimes you exaggerate a *lot* when you talk about fishing." She started smiling and giggled a little, and then she said, "But that tail in the back of the truck just proves you were telling the truth about the salmon that you and John let loose."

She then asked Cork what he was going to do with it. He told her he was going to preserve and mount it for John, but he hadn't figured out how, yet.

The next morning, while he was having coffee after his breakfast, the phone rang. It was Pat. He just wanted to remind Cork that he had forgotten to get paid for the bobber order that he had brought and that at the present time, his store was full of fish and game employees having breakfast.

Pat didn't say anything for a couple of seconds, because he knew Cork was going to ask. And he did. After sitting up straight in his chair, he said, "What have they been up to this morning? I'm sure the river and creeks are all over their banks."

Pat assured him that they were, but the people were looking for those bones that the fish and game lady had seen and measured the day before. He said, "They think maybe the bones might wash up on a bank or get tangled in some brush along the creek or river."

Cork, without thinking, said, "No, that couldn't happen, the bones are too heavy for that" and then having realized what he said, added, "at least I would think they would be if they are really that big."

Cork then told Pat he would be over in a couple of days and would stop in and get the check for the bobbers.

After Pat hung up the phone, he giggled to himself and thought, "that sneaky Old Bastard, he went and got those bones before the creek come up and I'll bet that old Johnathon Price went with him, too." He then burst out laughing, wondering what they were up to.

Cork sat there for a minute or two and thought over what Pat had said. He didn't think that he had done anything wrong. He couldn't remember any law saying that a person couldn't pick up a bone that he found and take it home. Now, if that fish had consumable meat on its carcass, that would be a different story. Besides, he felt that he and Johnathon had more right to those fish bones than the fish and game commission. Actually, he wasn't real sure about that, so he thought he had better keep his mouth shut, just in case they came and tried to take them away from him and Johnathon. Once John had them, he could do what he wanted, of course. That was up to him.

Cork went out to the pickup and lowered his tailgate to look at the tail. After studying it for a few minutes, he went to his shop for a meat saw. He decided to cut the backbone away, leaving about three or four inches attached to the tail. It would be easier to cut it on his tailgate than on the ground or trying to carry it to a table in his shop.

He finally finished the job. He stood there about half winded and looked at the backbone that he had cut off. Thinking that he was sure he would never see anything like it again in his life, and since he was a carver and liked to work on bones and antlers, he decided to dry it out and see what he could make out of it later.

He then grabbed the tail and carried it over to the water hose behind his barn, in his garden area, and tried to wash the mud and grime off it.

After doing this, he put it on a piece of plywood that he found in his woodshed and spread it out, tilting the board by placing a rock under one side so the water would run off.

He then went back to his shop and got a bag of rock salt that he used in preserving bait products. He figured that he would salt the tail down and leave it out in the sun to dry out.

He returned to his pickup, got the backbone, and laid it down next to the tail. He spread salt on it also.

Since he was in his fenced-in garden area and he could close the gates, he didn't think anything would bother the bones and tail. He could probably leave them there until a rainstorm came, and none was expected for a few days. When that happened, he would just pull them into the barn so they wouldn't get wet again.

The storm that had pounded the area in the last few days had blown itself out and moved east overnight. It was supposed to be warm and sunny, which would help in drying and preserving the bones.

He was confident that his dog and cats would leave them alone, but he wasn't sure of the blue jays and other birds that were around, although he wasn't really worried about it.

CHAPTER 51

Scott and Beth stopped at the Hebo Sporting Goods Store and had breakfast after they decided there was no use looking any further that day for the bones.

Scott asked Pat if he had heard the weather report. Pat told him that it wasn't supposed to rain again for a week or so, and if they were lucky, the rivers would start dropping since they had crested already. But it would probably take three or four days for them to get back into fishable condition.

As they were leaving, Scott told Pat that they would be back in a couple of days to continue their stream survey on some of the other tributaries, and by the time they were done with that, maybe the Big River would be down far enough for them to run their survey down from Moon Creek.

He also told Pat what had happened at the main office that morning and to expect a lot of publicity about the bones. He added that there could be a lot of people coming into the area looking for them, and not just people from the fish and game commission, either.

Pat said, "That would be like looking for a needle in a haystack." And then, smiling, he added, "At least it would be good for business. I really hope you find them, though. I would like to see them for myself."

As they were leaving the parking lot, Beth mumbled, "I don't think he believes me, just like everyone else."

After driving a short distance, Scott quietly said, "If it's any consolation, Beth, I do. For one thing, I've only known you for a couple of days, but I'm a pretty good judge of character. I know you wouldn't make up a story like that, and I also know you well enough to know that you didn't make a mistake in measuring or identifying those bones."

Beth looked at Scott. She said, "Thank you, Scott. I appreciate that."

After a short moment of silence, Scott looked at Beth out of the corner of his eye and said, "By the way, would you like to have dinner with me tonight?"

Beth's mouth fell open. And then, catching herself, she said, "Of course. Where, and what time?"

After Scott and Beth left the Nestucca Sporting Goods Store, Pat thought about what Scott had told him, and he immediately started taking inventory of his food stocks in his Deli. He realized that he was a little low on some of his food items, and if he was, in fact, swamped with customers as Scott predicted, he would definitely be in trouble. So he started to make an order list.

As it was, Scott was right. The next day and for many after, the Nestucca River Valley, below Moon Creek and all the way to Cloverdale, was overrun with people looking for the bones of the "Big Salmon of the Century," as stated by many newspapers, local and otherwise. There was even a rumor of a substantial reward put up by the fish and game commission and a couple of fishing organizations for the recovery of the bones.

Many fishermen came into Pat's store and complained of the people floating in boats and walking down the river, yelling, wading in and out of the water, crawling in the brush at the water's edge, and, in general, making it very hard to fish. There was even a fistfight reported between a searcher and a fisherman. More than a few of the fishermen said that they finally gave up and went home.

Even Pat, who had looked forward to the increase in business, got disgusted. After all, most of the people walking through his door didn't buy anything. They just wanted directions to Moon Creek or had some other question about the salmon bones and where to go look for them.

Sometimes his small parking lot was full, and cars were parking on the highway. He made the comment that it was getting to look like Grand Central Station, and cars were having a hard time passing through Hebo on the highway because it was so congested.

A lot of bones were found—dairy cow bones, deer bones, bones from about every small animal that inhabits a river were found. Even a few salmon carcasses were brought in to be photographed and measured, but none were of an extra-large Salmon.

Some of the dairy farmers bordering the river were getting concerned. A skin diver found a large salmon carcass in a body of water between Hebo and Cloverdale. He called his wife on his cell phone, and within a half hour, people were converging on the area he supposedly called from, at the bottom end of a dairy farm field. They never asked the farmer for permission to go through his gates and drive through his property. As it was, a few vehicles got stuck, and the farmer had to pull them out with his tractor.

It turned out, after examination by some biologists, that the bones were from a large salmon, but not that large, probably in the forty-pound range when alive, but far from the size of the fish that Beth had seen and measured.

The onslaught of humans in the in the Nestucca Valley lasted a little more than a week. By that time, the entire river from Moon Creek to Pacific City had been scoured and searched to no avail. No unusual or large salmon bones had been observed or found, and most people thought it was some kind of hoax, for publicity or some other reason.

Just about all the locals were glad to see the people leave, although there were no real problems except a fistfight or two down on the river between some of the searchers. The ones hoping to find the bones for the reward, who had drunk too much beer during their endeavor. Of course, the police had been called, but no arrests were made.

CHAPTER 52

Cork knew what was going on over on the river. He had been talking to Johnathon and Pat on the phone. Only one time during the two-week ordeal did he venture over the Coastal Mountains, and that was to retrieve the check he had forgotten to get from Pat for his bobbers.

He came around the corner in sight of the Highway 22 and Highway 101 junction, saw all the congestion, and decided not to attempt to reach Pat's store. He turned around and drove back to Johnathon's house.

When he reached Johnathon's driveway, Johnathon walked out to meet him, saying, "Did you drive down to the sporting goods store? My God, what a mess. And it's all your fault—you and those damned bones."

Cork said, "Me! If you would have kept that fish last fall instead of letting it go, this wouldn't be happening, and you know it."

"And just what do you think would be happening if I had done that?" said Johnathon. "Hell, Cork, all those people down there would be on my doorstep, and you know it."

It was quiet for a second or two, and then Cork smiled and said, "You're probably right." He paused for a second and then added, "And they still might be here if they hear the story and see those bones."

Johnathon wasn't smiling. "You wouldn't. You wouldn't do that, Cork." He looked Cork in the eye. "That would be an awful thing to do. They would come after you too, and you know it."

Cork, still smiling, said, "Be good to me, John," and he started chuckling.

John muttered, "You're still an asshole."

Cork got back in his pickup and said over his shoulder, "Since you're in such a fine mood this morning, I believe I'll head back over the mountain and say hello to Lucy." And he drove away, leaving Johnathon standing in his driveway with a frown on his face.

As Cork drove back out on Highway 22 and headed over the mountains, he thought, "What am I going to do with those bones?"

He had almost finished mounting them. It was quite a process.

He had used his power washer on them at first. But it had started to disconnect some of the small bones in the tail, so he had to stop and lightly scrub them with a small hand brush. After that, he let them dry and then put a light coating of salt all over and around them.

Leaving them out in the sun seemed to finish the preserving process.

While the bones were drying, Cork found a piece of one-half-inch plywood in his lumber pile that had one finished side. He sanded the finished side smooth and then stained it with a dark walnut stain, figuring it would contrast with the white bones.

He then cleaned all the salt from the tail, took it into his shop, and laid it out on a large piece of cardboard. Some of the bones had come loose and had to be superglued back into place.

When all was ready, he took a small paintbrush and started spreading liquid plastic over the exposed side of the bones.

After it dried, which was about twenty-four hours, he turned the tail over and spread liquid plastic on the other side.

He repeated this process three times, until the bones looked like they were encased in a covering of glass.

Then he placed them on the stained piece of plywood, drilled through the back of the plywood, and attached the tail bones in four different places with stainless-steel screws that could not be seen from the front.

After it was done, he stood back and looked at it. He wasn't satisfied. To him, it still looked like a bunch of bones. So he took a large silver marker and outlined what the tail should have looked like in the flesh, and then, liking what he had done, colored in between the bones with the marker.

After doing all this and satisfied with how it looked, he sprayed the entire project with polyurethane three times.

Linda had seen the bones when Cork first arrived home with them but had not seen what he was doing to them in his shop, so when Cork was finished and the last coat of polyurethane had dried, he went and got her.

When she saw the mounted salmon tail, her eyes got big, and she was speechless. She had not expected to see what she was looking at.

She turned to Cork and said, "My gosh, honey, that turned out beautiful." She wanted to know just how he had done it, and he told her.

He asked her if she thought John would like it, and she told him that if he didn't, to bring it back home and she would put it up in the house.

As she was talking, she was examining every inch of it, like she always did with things he made. He knew that if she found something she didn't like or a flaw, she would immediately tell him, like she always did. It was kind of a standing joke between them. Apparently it passed inspection, because she never said anything.

CHAPTER 53

Cork had been talking to Johnathon and Pat on the phone, and about a week after the influx of bone hunters left the Nestucca River area, Cork decided to take the tail down to John. He also threw in one of the vertebrae, which he had kept in the freezer. He had planned on drying them out and trying to carve some type of picture on them later. He thought maybe John would want to try one himself, since he was a carver also.

Of course, as luck would have it, Johnathon wasn't home but down at Pat's having a cup of coffee, according to Lucy, so Cork went on down to the store.

To his surprise when he walked in the door, he encountered more than Johnathon and Pat. There were two fish and game employees and an older gentleman sitting at one of the tables across from Johnathon. Pat was at the counter, as usual.

They all looked over at him as he entered, and the store got immediately quiet. Pat said that he had called his home, and Linda had informed him that he was on the way over.

Cork gave Pat a questioning look, and Pat just shrugged and nodded at the people with Johnathon at the table.

Cork walked over to them, and one of the fish and game employees, with the green jacket showing the fish and game patch on the shoulder, stood up.

It was a young woman, and Cork recognized her and her partner as the ones who had been in the store a month or so ago. She was the one who had blurted out that she had measured a salmon tail that was thirty-two inches and started the whole amazing drama of the last few weeks.

She asked, "Are you Cork Lofton?"

Cork nodded yes but didn't say anything. He looked at Johnathon, who was looking down at his feet, which gave him an urge to turn around and walk back out the door.

She said, "My name is Beth Roberts." Turning to the young man on her right, she said, "This is Scott Dale, my partner." And then, looking at the older man, "And this is my dad, Dan Roberts, who is a biologist with the federal government."

Cork nodded at each man as she introduced him.

She then asked, "Do you remember seeing my partner, Scott, and me in the store a while back and me mentioning a measurement that I took of a salmon tail up on Moon Creek?"

Cork answered, "Yes, ma'am, I sure do." And then, smiling slightly, he added, "I bet now you wish you had never said that, huh?"

Beth, who up to that time had been all straight faced and businesslike, grinned and immediately took a liking to Cork, who reminded her of her dad, who was sitting not far away with a frown on his face. She said in a low voice, "That's for sure!"

She then said, "I understand from rumors coming from all over this area that you might know something about the tail bones in question."

Cork quit smiling and looked over at Johnathon, who looked like a pooch who had just been yelled at or whupped.

He said, "John, what have you told them? Would you like to go outside and discuss this?"

Johnathon was starting to answer when Dan Roberts came unglued. He jumped up from his seat, red in the face, and said, rather loudly, "Lofton, if you know anything about this f——in' mess, I want to know about it right now. My daughter is about to lose her job, and her reputation as a fish biologist is probably ruined forever just because of these damned bones. So if you know anything about it, you had better tell us, or so help me, you are going to be sorry."

Cork was usually a pretty mellow and even-tempered fellow, but if there was one thing he didn't stand for, it was being threatened. And another thing was being cussed at in front of other people, especially females. He didn't know this man who was talking, and for sure the man didn't know Cork or know much about him, or he would never have said what he did.

Cork looked Dan Roberts in the eye and commenced to tell him to control himself, and if he couldn't do so in the store, maybe he would like to go outside and continue the conversation.

Johnathon, knowing Cork as well as he did, knew where this was heading. It took a little while for Cork to come to a boiling point, but his eyes were slits, and the veins on his temple were standing out, and that was not a good sign.

He stood up and gently took Cork by the right arm and said, "Let's talk about this." And he led him out the door.

When they got outside, Cork said, "I don't like that guy!"

Johnathon said, "Oh, really? Well, I guess everyone in there knows that, huh?"

Cork then asked Johnathon what he had told them, and he said, "Not much. Just that we heard about the bones and went looking for them on Moon Creek—which, by the way, they already had heard about." He then went on and told him that he never said anything about finding them and never said anything about catching and releasing the big fish last fall.

Cork, who had calmed down, said, "You know, John, I've had about enough of this crap. Why don't we tell them all about the fish and the bones. And, by the way, I have the bones with me in the pickup. I was bringing them to you. That's what I'm doing down here."

Johnathon, looking down at the ground, didn't say anything for a few seconds. And then he said, "Well, if you really think we should. But you know what's going to happen, don't you? Our worst fears are going to come true. People are going to hound us to death."

He then asked Cork, "Hell, you're the retired cop. Have we done anything that's against any law that you know about?"

"Not that I'm aware of, but John, there are so many new ones anymore that I can't be sure."

Cork said, "They may try to take the bones away from us, and that's where it might get sticky-icky. I'm not going to let that happen. We found them, and we're going to keep them."

He then went quiet, thinking for a second before adding, "John, they already have a pretty good idea that we have them. They might even try to get a search warrant to get them, although I don't think there is a judge in the country that would issue one on hearsay evidence, which is all they have. But what I'm trying to say is that we could never show them off. We would have to destroy them or hide them forever, which is just stupid."

Both men went quiet and then Jonathon said, "OK, let's do it. We'll show it to them, and maybe it'll turn out all right. I trust the girl, but I don't trust her dad."

Cork said, "Me either."

CHAPTER 54

When Johnathon and Cork walked back into the store, it was dead quiet. More people had entered the store in their absence, some local and some not. Eight more, to be exact, which included Chuck Rowland and Mel, who had stopped at the store because they recognized Cork's and John's vehicles parked back in the rear and the fish and game vehicle parked in the front.

Apparently, after Cork and Johnathon had gone outside, Pat had told Beth's dad that he did not allow any disturbances like the one he had just witnessed in his store, and if he couldn't conduct himself in a professional manner without the use of profanity, then he had better go outside with Cork and Johnathon to continue their conversation.

As Cork entered, he looked around at all the people, nodding at the ones he knew or recognized. He then stopped, placed his hands on Pat's glass counter, and said to all the people who were staring at him, "Well, I'm getting set to tell a story. But first I want to ask the ones from the government whether they plan on trying to confiscate the fish bones, if they ever see them."

Dan Roberts, looking rather sheepish and red in the face after Pat's admonishment, said, "No. I just want to verify my daughter's measurement of the fish tail so all the rumors of false statements on official documents can be absolved."

Scott said that he didn't think that there would be any reason for the fish and game department to take the bones, but he did think that they would sure like to examine them, not only to verify Beth's measurement but to do scientific tests for DNA and such.

Beth, who had been listening to her dad and Scott, just sat still with a hopeful look on her face and shook her head no.

Cork said, "OK then, here it goes." And he started telling his small audience about his and Johnathon's experience with the big female Chinook salmon the previous fall on the Nestucca River.

There was only one interruption during the first part of the story—when Johnathon and Cork had the big fish up close and were touching her.

Beth stopped Cork and asked if they had had a chance to measure any part of the female Chinook before they released her.

Cork looked at Beth for a second and then, smiling, said, "Yes, we did, just before releasing her. She measured eighty and one-half inches from nose to tail." He then was quiet as everyone in the room absorbed what he had just said.

The only one who so much as uttered a peep was Dan Roberts, who said, rather quietly, "bullshit" and then looked down at his feet when he noticed Pat staring at him.

Cork just gave him a dirty look and continued with the story.

He said that when he heard Beth tell how she had measured a spawned-out salmon tail up on Moon Creek that was so big, well, he had to see for himself. So, after getting John, he went to find it.

He explained how they came close to losing their lives because the water was swift and coming up so fast. In fact, they almost let it go, but John held on, and he held on to John, and they finally made it out with the bones.

It took about a half hour to tell the story, and when he was finished, he just stood there and looked at the group, who were looking back at him, seemingly rather spellbound.

All were quiet, but then Dan Roberts opened his mouth and said, "That's a good story, Lofton, and I'm sure my daughter appreciates it. But where are the bones now? I suppose you lost them or something."

Cork just looked at him, thinking, That guy must have been in a lot of fights growing up with that attitude. He had a big urge to walk over and pop him in the snot locker in front of all those people. And he was sure most of them expected him to do that, but he didn't. Instead, he said, "Well, just so happens that I was on the way to John's house when I walked in here. Just stay where you are, and I'll be right back." And he walked out the door.

When he returned, he was carrying the mounted tail. It wasn't easy, because of the size and weight, but he got it through the door backward. And when he turned it around in front of the group, there were a whole bunch of wide eyes and mouths hanging open.

A bunch of bones isn't a very pretty sight, but what Cork had done with them by encasing them in plastic and then outlining them with the markers so they looked like an actual tail was beautiful.

Even Pat was impressed, and that took some doing. He muttered, "Wow, that's huge."

Cork stood the mount up and, with Pat's help, held it on the counter while the people tried to get a closer look at it. Some were taking pictures with their cell phones.

Beth took some with Scott holding a yardstick that he had gotten from Pat in front of the tail, and so did Dan Roberts.

All was going well until Dan Roberts said, "Lofton, I agreed to not try to take the bones, but I will have to renege because we have to get some samples for examination. And the only way I can see to do that is to cut into them at the lab."

The whole group immediately went hostile, including Scott and Beth, when Cork said that he had figured something like that would happen and walked back out the door, leaving Pat to hold up the mount by himself.

When he returned, he was carrying a ziploc plastic bag with one of the fish's vertebrae in it. He handed it to

Beth, told her what it was, and told her if her dad wanted any samples from it, he was going to have to be awful nice to her, Scott, and the Oregon Game Commission.

Beth took the bag, looked at it for a second, and then, after glancing at Scott, who was smiling, and then at her dad, who was not, turned back to Cork. With tears starting to run down her cheeks, she threw her arms around him and kissed him on the cheek, saying, "Oh, thank you Mr. Lofton."

AFTERMATH

When Cork returned home from Hebo, he told Linda what had happened and told her to pack. They were going on a trip for a week or so.

He asked the neighbors to watch and feed their dog and cat, and they left in about an hour.

Their cell phones rang many times, but they didn't answer them except when they saw it was from one of their children or grandchildren.

Finally, after three days, Johnathon called, and Cork answered it. The first thing Johnathon said was to call Cork an asshole for leaving, and then, after he was done laughing, he told Cork about all the people in Hebo and in and out of his door, taking pictures of the mount and asking him questions.

This lasted for days, weeks, and even years, just like Cork had predicted.

Even when he returned home, he was confronted by hordes of writers, reporters, and people who just wanted to talk about the incident.

Pat and the sporting goods store in Hebo were also in the limelight and set upon by many people who just wanted to be in the area and talk about the largest Chinook salmon in history. Pat and his wife, Lori, must have told the story, as they had heard it, a couple of hundred times, at least.

Cork still had six dried vertebrae from the large fish, two of which he carved small versions of Chinook salmon on. He mounted them on pieces of plasticized driftwood that he and Linda had found on the beach. He had one sitting on a shelf in his office, and he gave the other to Beth and Scott, who, incidentally, had become extremely attracted to each other and eventually got married.

They had two children, a boy and a girl, two years apart. And guess who the god grandfathers were. Cork even made Johnathon wear a tie.

A year or so after the large salmon incident, it was rumored that during trout season, some Chinook salmon smolt were caught that measured a foot in length, which is totally unheard of. This caused a flurry of activity around the fish and game office and sent many biologists and their aides to the Nestucca River area to investigate, but to no avail. No large smolt were found and recorded.

As Jonathon Pierce put it to a writer for a fish and game magazine at a public interview, "I guess time will only tell, folks." And then he looked over at Cork and smiled great big.

Two Old Men and A Fish

Cork and 54lb Chinook

Cork and Ray, average fall Chinook limit on the Nestucca river

Linda and 48lb Chinook

Two Old Men and A Fish

Linda and 42lb Chinook

Made in the USA
Columbia, SC
09 November 2024

45810896R00163